# The Christmas Cards

This is a work of fiction. Similarities to persons, living or dead, are neither intended nor should be inferred.
For more information, please visit www.darkfluidity.com



ISBN: 0-9983882-0-3
ISBN-13: 978-0-9983882-0-5

Created by
DarkFluidity

in Association with

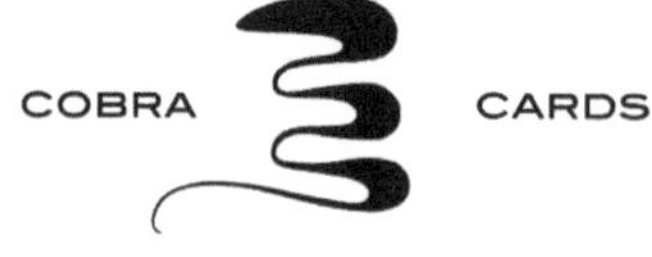

# The Christmas Cards

artwork: Mery-et Lescher

words: John Urbancik

# DEDICATION

To our Christmas card list.

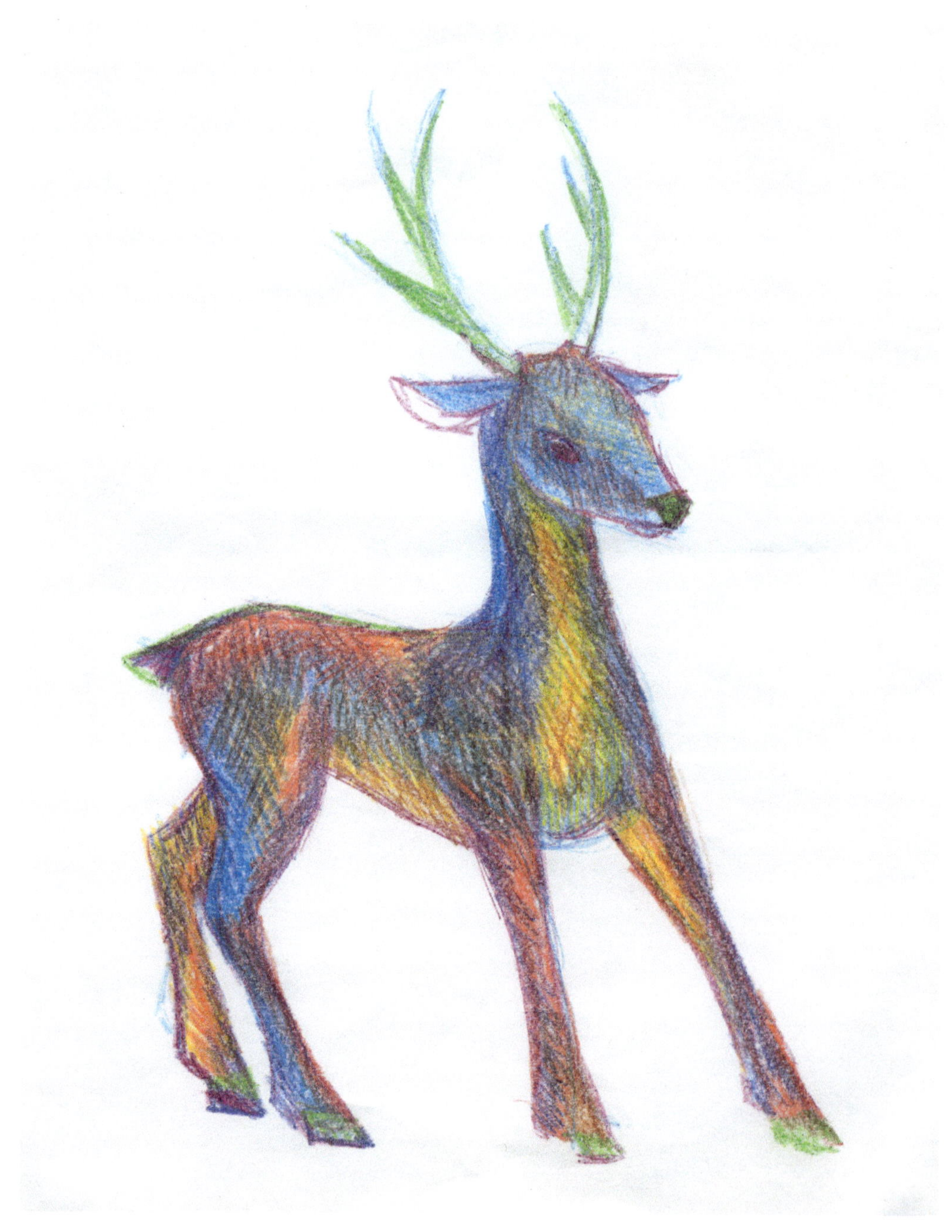

2009

# INTRODUCTION

Each year, people tell us how much they love receiving a new card and story for the holidays. They tell me how they collect all my cards. My sister-in-law likes the Christmas Seals (1991). John's favorite may be the Southern Cross (2004). My favorite is...well...there are some I like more than others (1989, 1986, or 1999).

I began drawing Christmas cards around 1982 or 83 while working for a special-effects company, X-Group Productions, in New York City. From the start, I sought to make each image unique, individually hand-crafted. It was my act of creation that was the gift of the card. I played with various media—some worked, others didn't. All were handmade. I found certain media appealed more to me; these days, when academic papers are due and laundry calls, I tend to draw for the fun of those materials I favor. Of course, there's also the design itself, which dictates certain media.

When John and I began going out, he saw my Christmas card tradition and, being the wordsmith he is, started adding a short, short story to go out each year. (Some of my favorites include *The Forgotten Mailbox* and *The Sylvester Bros. Traveling Christmas Show & Extravaganza.*) The cards and stories were never designed with each other in mind; they are individual acts of creation. As for my hand-made tradition, I finally had to put an end to it when some of the designs became so complex it took days to create a single image! When there is lead-time, I still make a few colour models, but since starting Graduate School, I haven't had much time for drawing lately. (I have included some of these cards in their multiple colour versions.)

This might be why John and I have been talking about the creation of this book for so long. Yet, with the passing of each Winter Solstice, we look at each other, roll our eyes, and make mental notes to get started on the book early next year. It's like that "perfect fitness" urge one gets at the end of each year. This time, though, it seems John is finally going through with it. So here is evidence of our annual contribution of wit and image: a compilation of words and visuals inspired by feelings, drawn from secular and spiritual issues, that often emerge as nostalgia, tradition, and yes—a hint of indulgence. As creatives, John and I already have new dreams of what we might accomplish in the coming years, but this book presents evidence of those earlier moments.

Is it possible we feel more deeply at this time of year? Is it because after another twelve months have passed, we need to remember our inner selves and our unity with family and the community? We hope you will enjoy our little offering. Namaste.

– Thoughts by MEL
December 2015

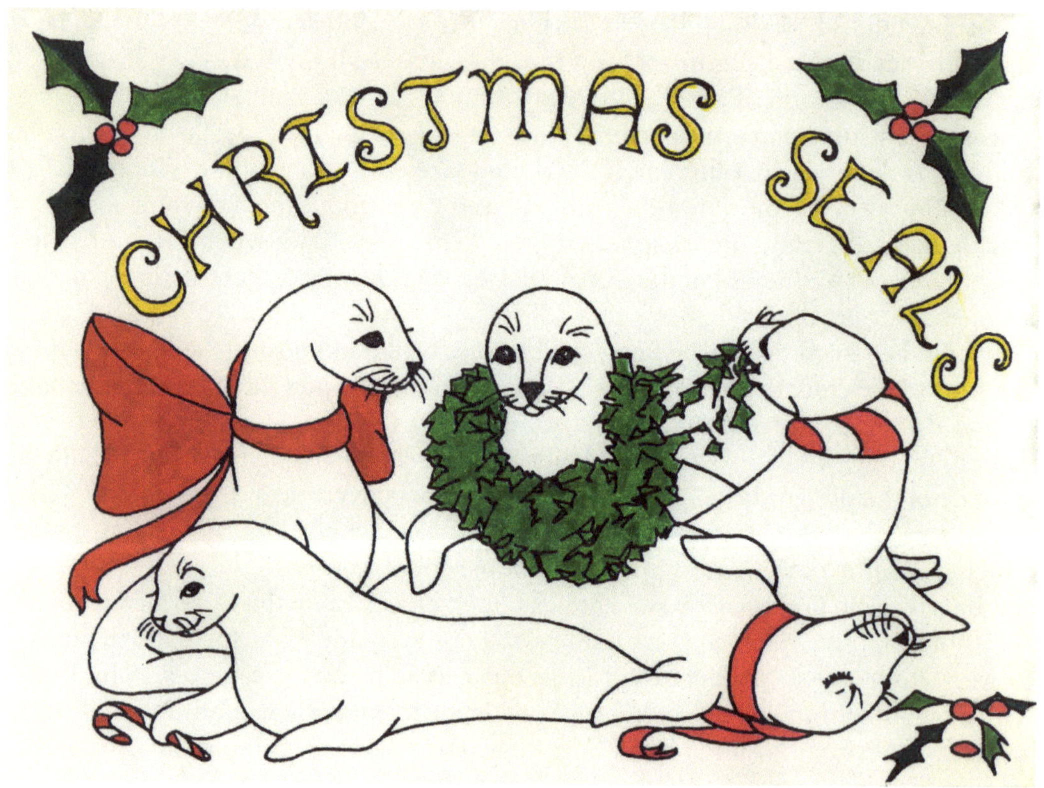
CHRISTMAS SEALS

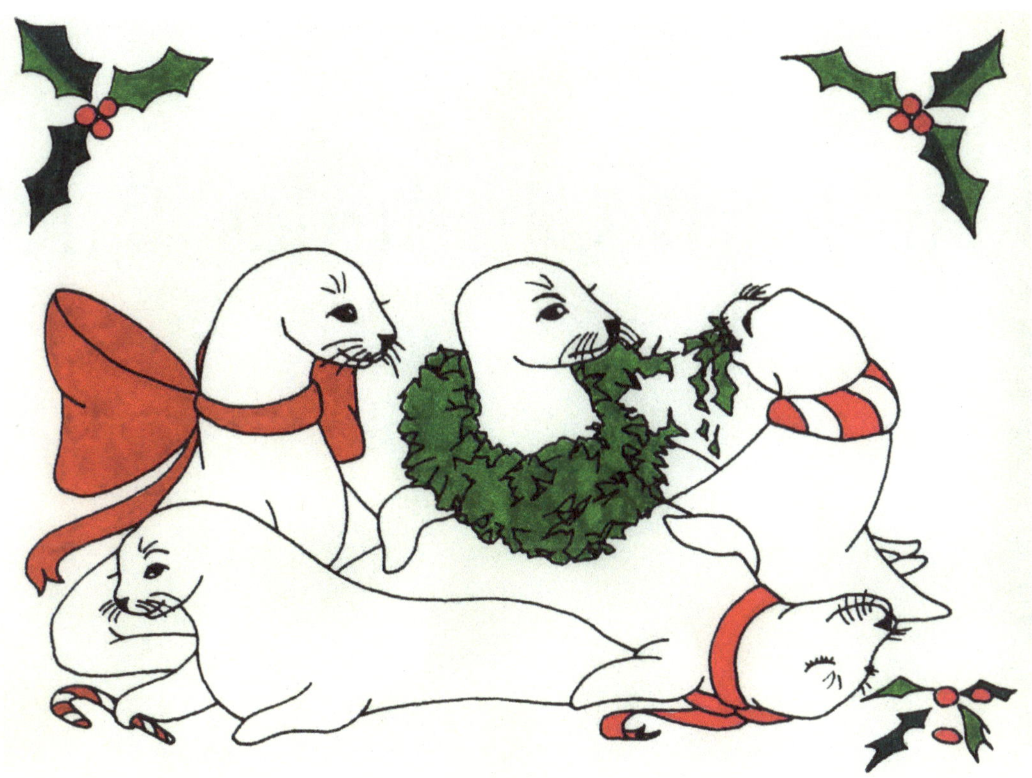

1991

# An Early Christmas Tale

1999

Nicholas watched the star. It signaled the start of something.

Instinct suggested he follow the star. But even by elven standards, Nicholas was old. He instead bundled his tools and went into the woods.

The younger elves, always curious, asked what he was doing and where he was going. All he could say was, "I don't know."

Animals, even those normally hibernating, gathered. It was a rare sight, an elf sitting in the snow and staring at the sky. Swallows flew about one day, disappeared for a night, and returned with a warm, crimson suit for Nicholas.

He thanked the birds and waited.

Three elves, with the help of Nicholas' wife, built him a sleigh. "Carry your sacks on this," they said. It easily held both him and all his tools. He thanked them.

A bear, usually asleep now, offered to pull the sleigh. "But I don't yet know where I'm going."

"When you're ready," said the bear.

The star burned bright, lighting the night in a way the moon often dreamed of doing. Days after the solstice, Nicholas learned in a dream where he should go. When he asked for the bear to pull his sleigh, a dozen reindeer came to help instead.

The harnesses only had space for eight, so the others pulled smaller sleds and the young elves who came with him. They traveled for twelve nights through the snow before reaching their destination. On the last night, the reindeer learned to fly.

Nicholas, a maker of toys, taught his art to the younger elves. Every year, when that star shines once more in the southern sky, Nicholas loads all they've made onto his sleigh and travels across the earth to distribute their toys. He was told to do this in his dreams. And there is, after all, only so much room at the North Pole.

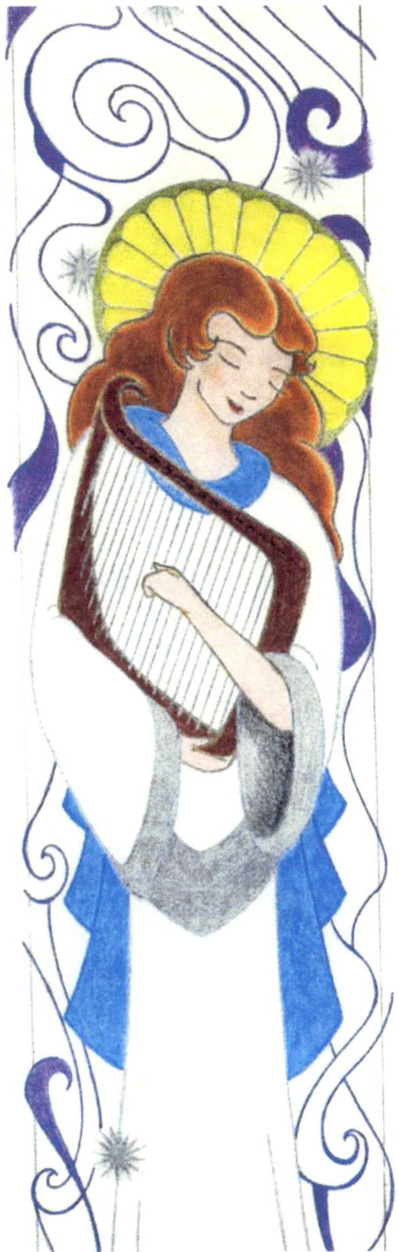

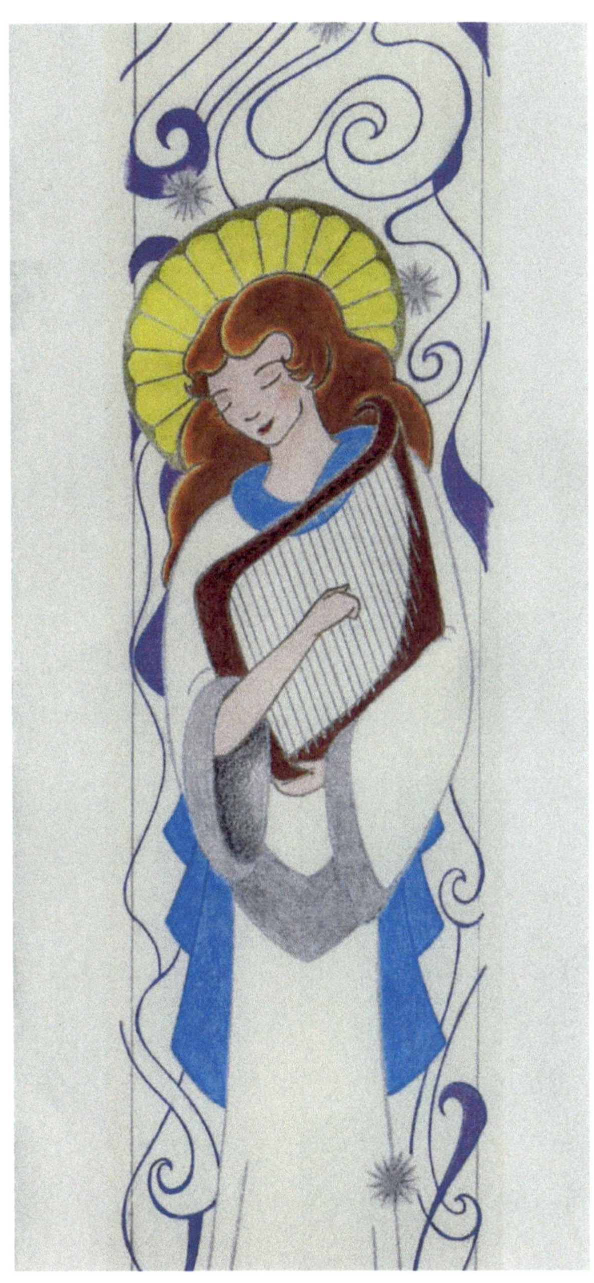

2002

# A Christmas Tale

2000

One star, alone, shining more brightly than maybe any star before, never knew where he led kings.

His had been a good life, and as it neared its end, a genie visited him.

Once, perhaps, this genie had lived in a bottle. Maybe that's how he knew of the earth, far away as it was. "Three wishes," he said to the star, "before you burn out."

"Then these," said the star. "Peace and joy for a whole world full of people."

"That's two," said the genie. "Be careful what you choose."

"Two?"

The genie, feeling generous, said, "How about if I give a planet one day, perhaps seven or twelve, in which to celebrate peace and joy. That, for you, I will count as one."

"Agreed," said the star. So he made his next wish: "I want children across the galaxy to be happy."

"Again," said the genie, "that's quite an enormous task. How about if I give the children of one planet a time to give and receive gifts and happiness? A day, perhaps seven or twelve, devoted to nothing else."

"Children," said the star, "of all ages."

"Agreed," said the genie. "But your wishes, thus far, have been so altruistic. Don't you want anything for yourself?"

"If you think I should," the star said, and he paused to think. "I just want to be remembered after I'm gone."

"That," said the genie, "can be done." He helped ease the star out of life with a brilliant flash that, eventually, would be seen throughout the galaxy.

Millennia later, for a relatively short period of time, the star burned so brightly in earth's sky, it led kings, wisemen, and shepherds to a child.

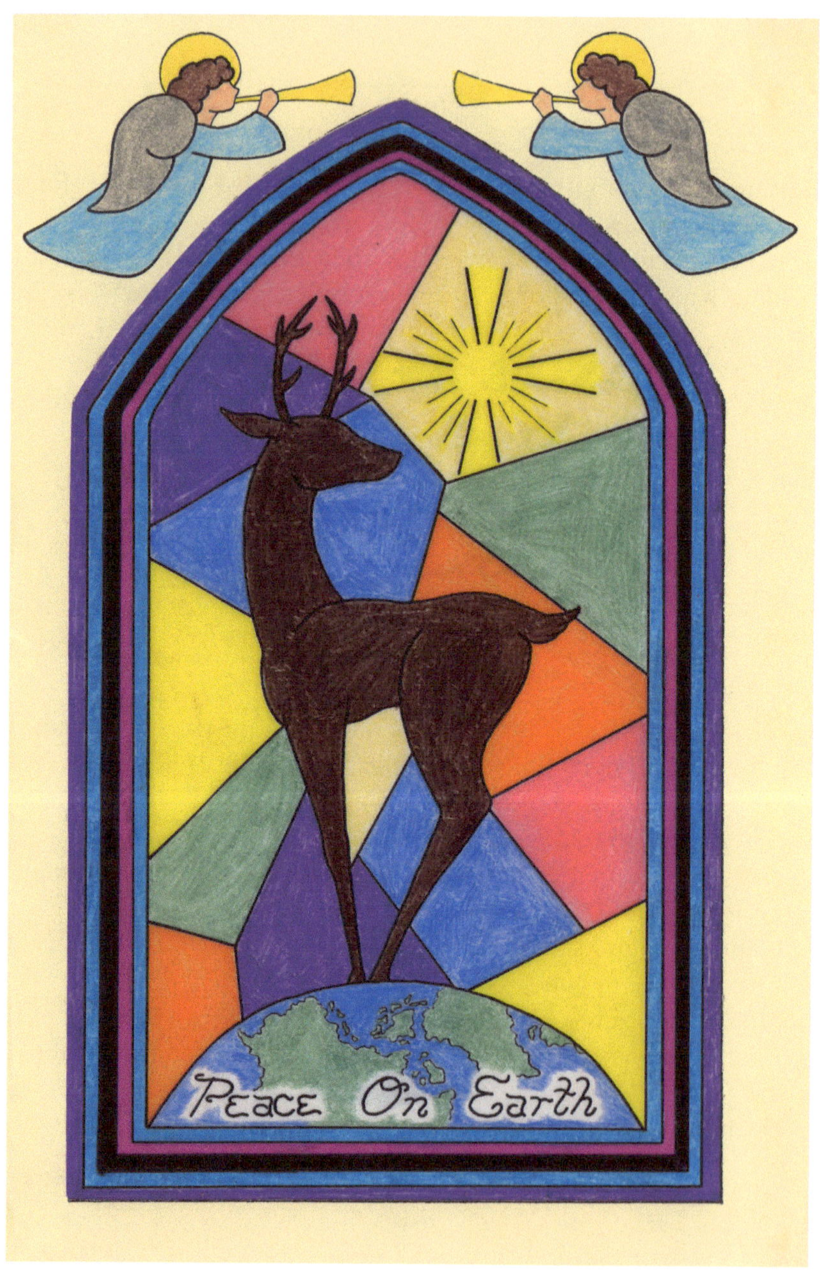
Peace On Earth

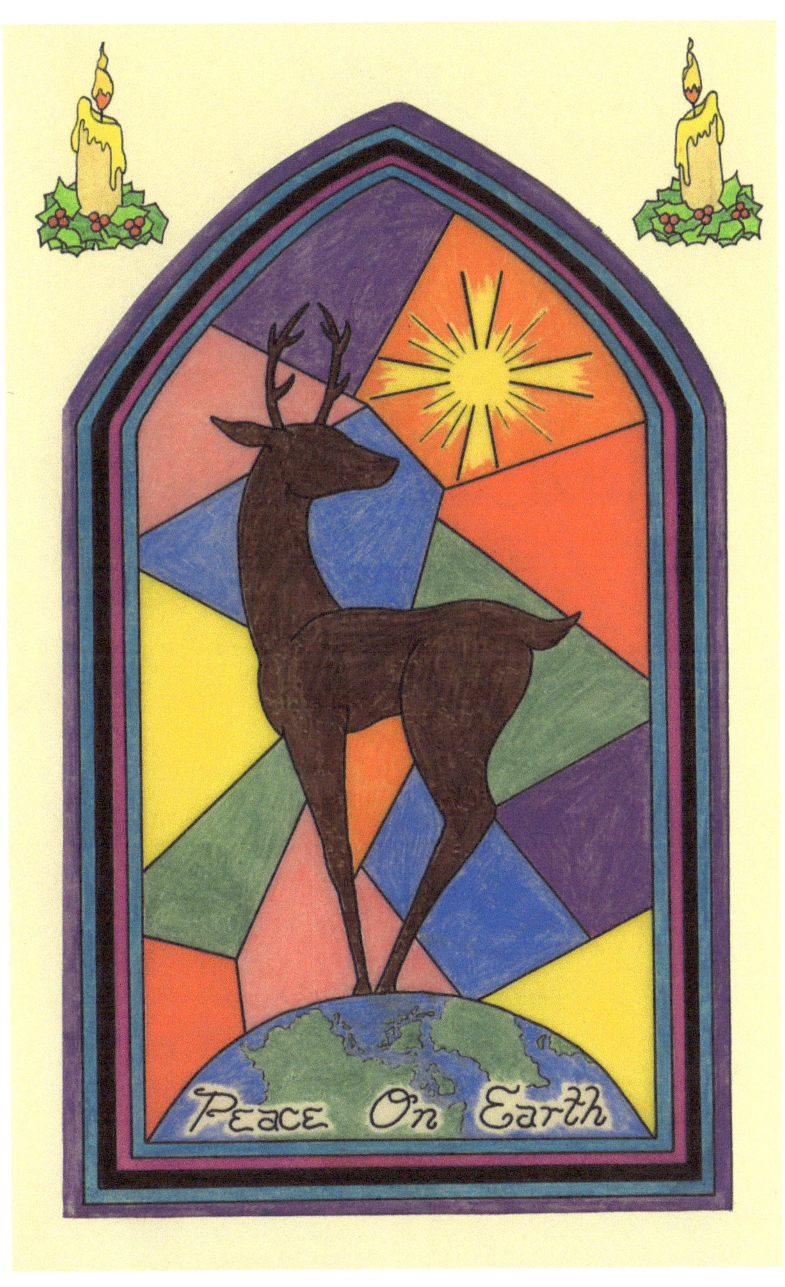


1993

# Once Upon a Christmas Eve

2001

*Slightly less than two thousand years ago:*

On the warmest winter days, you can sometimes watch icicles drip outside the window. It's too cold to be out there, underneath, catching the water on your tongue like a snowflake, but Christopher stares through the spider web of frost on his window and remembers the winters of long ago.

He knows he should be working. It's been a long day on the far end of a long month, but there are the children to remember. He makes toys. Wood dust and driplets of paint coat his workshop. The parents want toys to give to their children, to celebrate the new holiday. He understands what they want, and why, but not why they want so much of it *from him*. He's just one man. His muscles ache. His bones are tender. His wife, bless her, has been ever patient, but for how much longer?

He sighs, gives up his icicle, and returns to his task. It is, after all, joyous work. His father, and his father before him, worked this trade. It's a special talent. A gift. His father once said only a drop of magic in the blood makes it possible for a person to be a toymaker. Christopher's son, one day, will also make a fine toymaker.

He picks up his tools (which he keeps in a leather pouch) and begins another doll. He can create ten–maybe twelve–in a day. Others may make more, but the difference is that of the words *make* and *create*. The parents know this, and the children know.

But because of the time and energy, the sweat and, yes, sometimes blood–because of all this, Christopher cannot possibly meet the demand for his toys.

He falls asleep in his workshop clutching an unfinished doll. Her smile has been drawn, but not painted.

The midnight hour arrives, and midnights often bring a taste of magic themselves. Combined with the blood that runs through Christopher's veins, magical stuff because of his father's father's ancestors–and maybe because of the nature of his task–and certainly because of some divine intervention...

Suffice it to say his are not the only veins that carry magic. The elves arrive in the moments after midnight. They sing and dance, eat and drink. They celebrate the efforts of this toy maker, this Christopher Kringle, and with magic they finish his work, leaving only the smile of the one doll for Christopher to finish in the morning.

They are there, still, when the toymaker wakes. "Ah, but we will help you," says one of the elves, "every year from now until you can work no more."

Christopher smiles. His wife finds them, her husband and the elves, in the workshop, and asks, "But, why?" Another of the elves, a pretty one with golden hair, curtseys and says, "Because toys are much more fun to create than shoes."

Season's

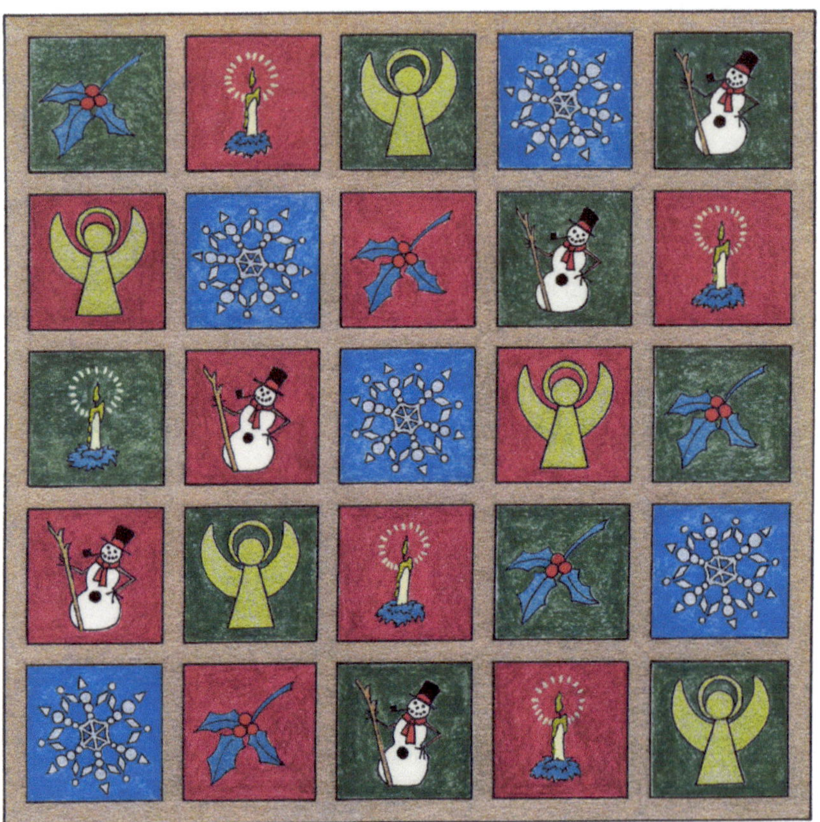

Greetings

2006

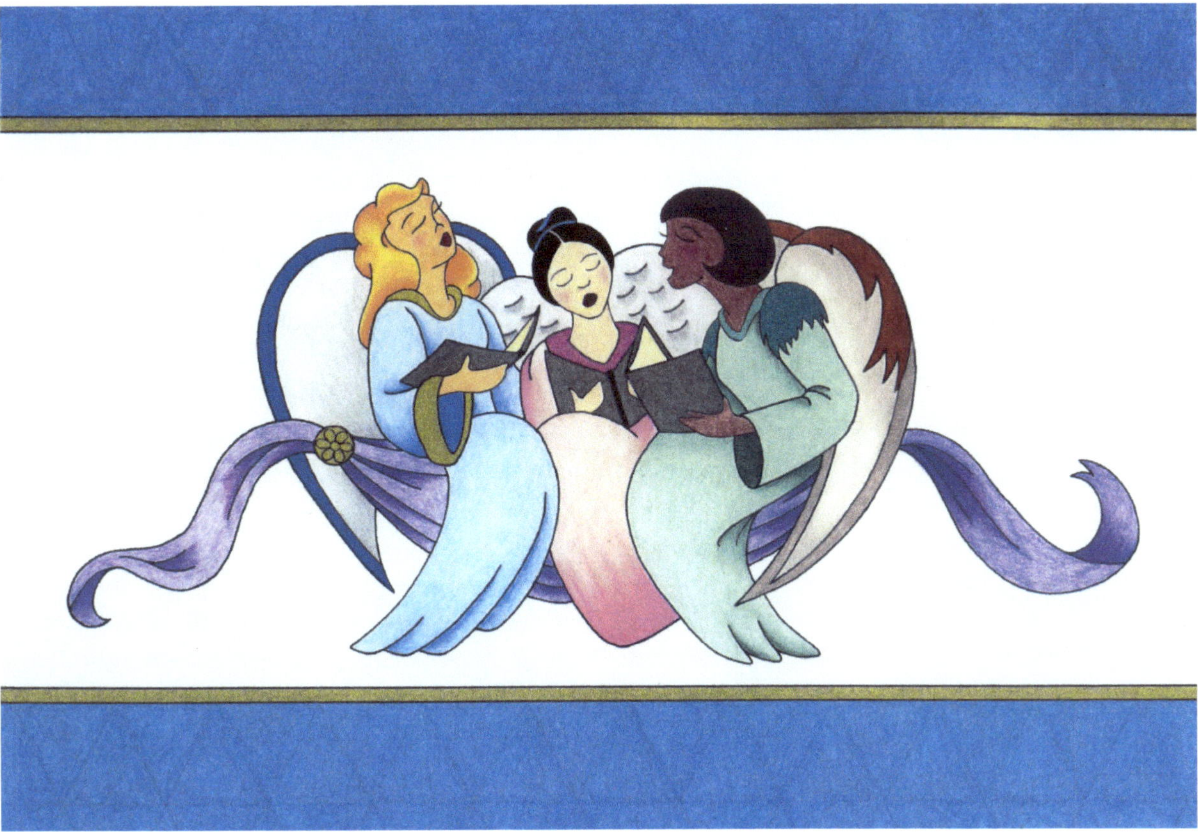

2005

# The Christmas Spirit

2002

A spirit.

Not the Ghost of Christmas Past, Present, or Future. Not a ghost of Christmas at all.

But a man who became a ghost one Christmas Eve.

He doesn't haunt. Doesn't even talk. Mostly, he watches. It's the kids opening presents that he most enjoys, the glee on their faces.

It's been a long time since he found a toy soldier Christmas morning. He's never heard of Rudolph or Frosty. Holidays were spent with family and cozy fires in the hearth, hot cocoa and turkey dinners.

He's just a spirit.

He doesn't watch the children anymore. It's not that they're so different—they still drink hot chocolate and make huge Christmas feasts—but he's found a way to more thoroughly enjoy the holiday.

For the kids, it's the anticipation. For the parents, too, the anticipation of their children's joy—and their own, private joys. This is what he loves most.

So he skips from house to house, watching the late night preparations of children (*one last appeal to St. Nick*), the parents (*some assembly required*), and the jolly old man in the big red suit.

He believes he's found the Spirit of Christmas. But he's wrong: he is that spirit.

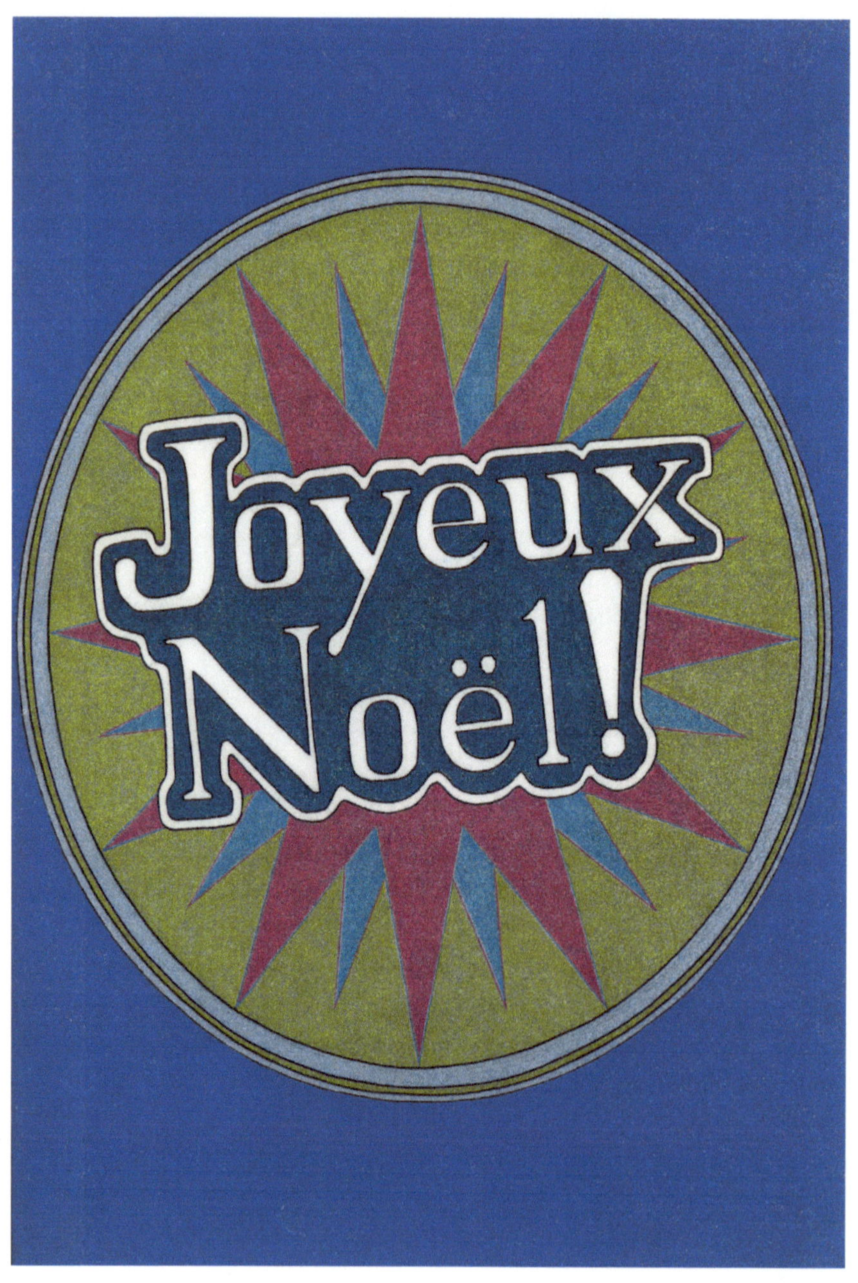


2013

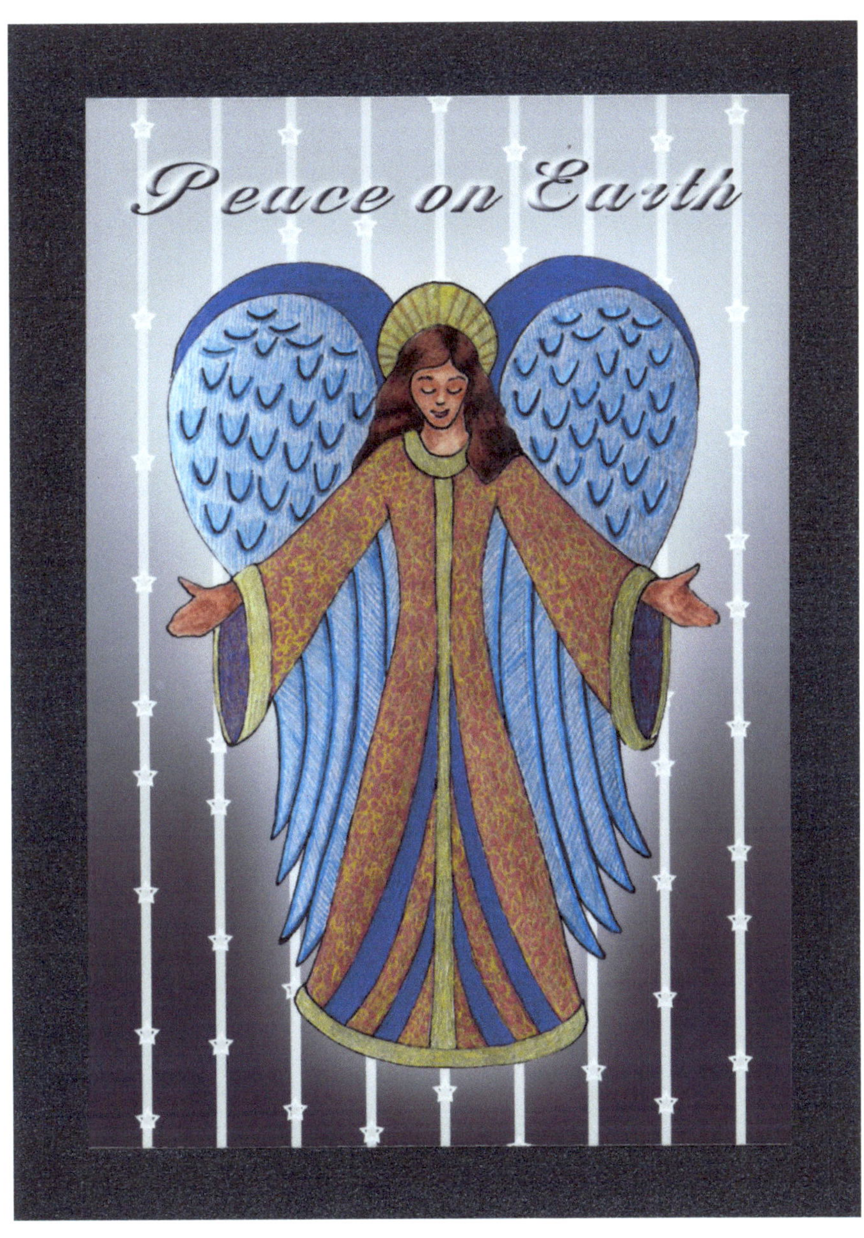


2012

# One Christmas Eve

2003

A ghost, sure, why not? I woke long after midnight to find a ghost eating cookies in my kitchen. Drinking a glass of milk. Leaning back on two legs of the chair and reading the comics.

"Brought it in for you," the ghost said, re-folding the paper. "Hope you don't mind." Bit a cookie, sipped his milk, stared unrelentingly at me. "Takes a lot to wake you, doesn't it?" He winked, grinning. "You sleep like the dead."

"I heard glass," I told him, recalling the tinkling sound that had roused me.

The ghost nodded. "Bathroom mirror. Terribly sorry about that."

He'd been my business partner. Echoes of Dickens ran through my mind, though my ghost wore no chains and I could never have been called a Scrooge.

"Am I to get three visitors?" I asked.

"You?" He laughed. "Funny. You're the guy who gives cows to poor African villages in the name of your rich friends. Bought a turkey dinner for six needy families this year."

"Three," I corrected him.

"Don't forget Thanksgiving," he said. "Wasn't that long ago. And that toy drive you run at the office..."

"That was your idea," I reminded him. Before the accident seven years ago.

"Perhaps," he said, "but this year's drive brought in double what you got last year."

"So," I said, sitting across from the ghost, "what brings you to my table this Christmas Eve?"

He finished the milk, wiped his mouth with the back of his hand, and said, "You want an honest answer, old friend?"

"Of course."

"You died in your sleep," the ghost said.

I nodded. I was old, it could've happened any time, and only when he said it did I realize all my normal aches were absent.

"So," the ghost said, standing and spreading his wings, "I'm recruiting Christmas Angels."

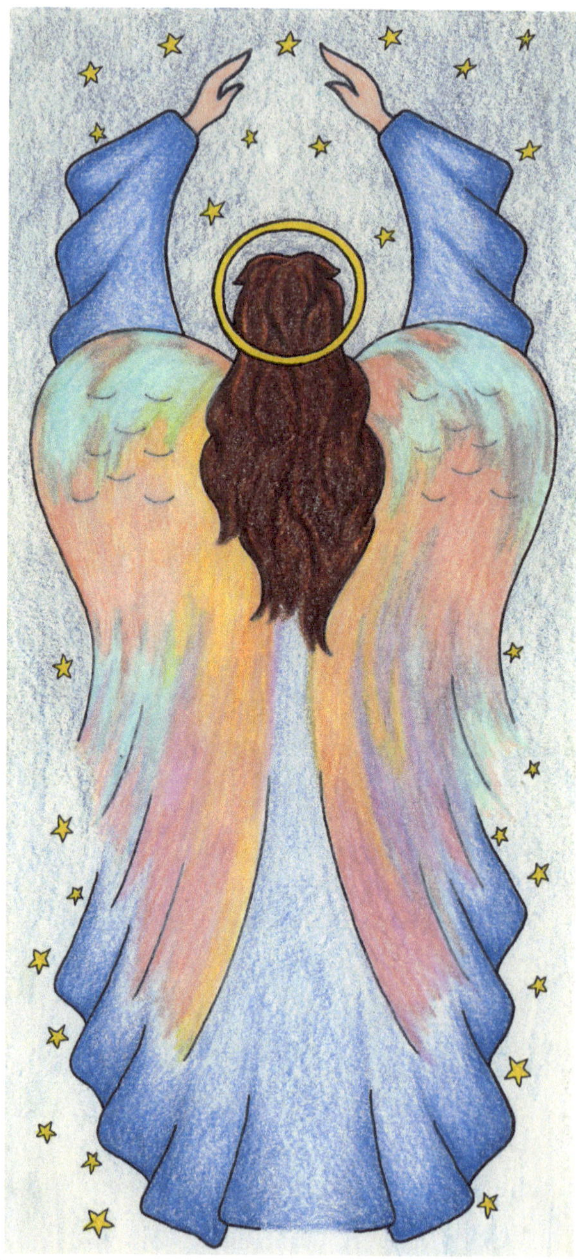

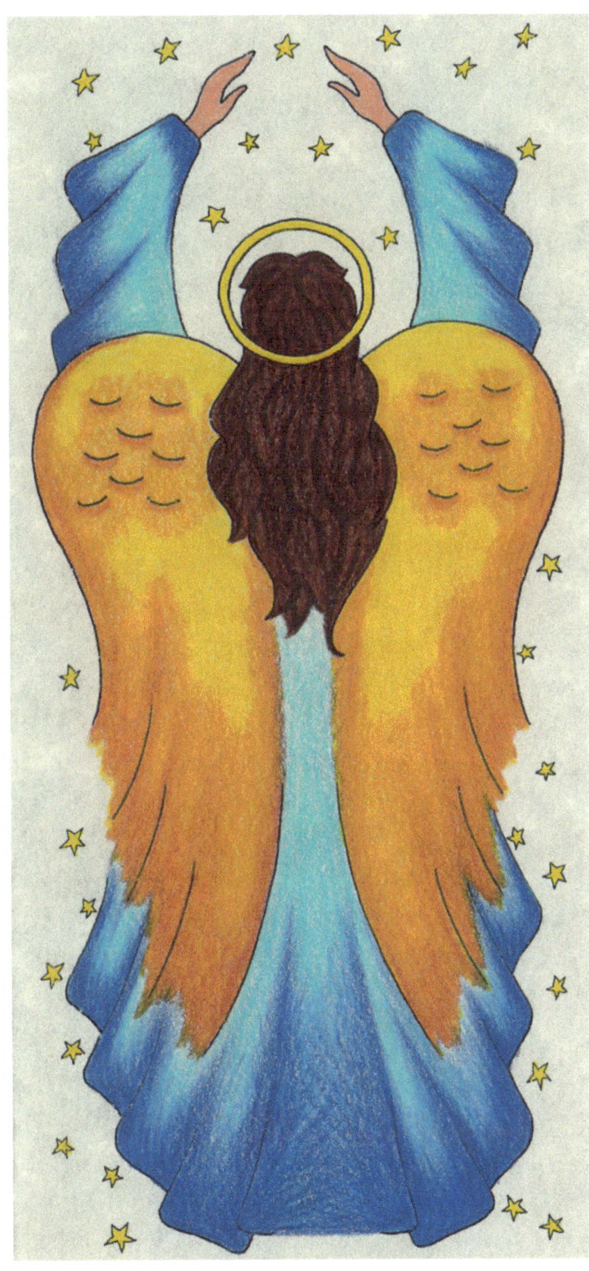

1989

# A Christmas Letter

2004

Dearest Friend,

You don't feel the cold while you're working. There's too much to do. Lists to check, orders to fill, toy soldiers to build (or video games, today, those seem quite popular).

And it's a busy season. I consider ourselves fortunate that not everybody celebrates, or not on the same day. Harry takes care of his own people, Grandfather Frost takes care of his, just as my Kris takes care of ours.

It's a fantastic job. None better in the world. I know he loves it.

But after the season, when there's not much work to do, when the lists have all been discarded and it's too early to start reporting on next year...well, the kids at school get a summer vacation, don't they? So why not my Kris?

Sure, it's winter up here, but that doesn't matter. And he won't get out of it this time.

I've got his swimming trunks packed, sunglasses and tanning lotion, even those wide-brimmed hats. I hear it gets mighty hot this time of year on those beaches in Australia.

Yours,

Mrs. Claus

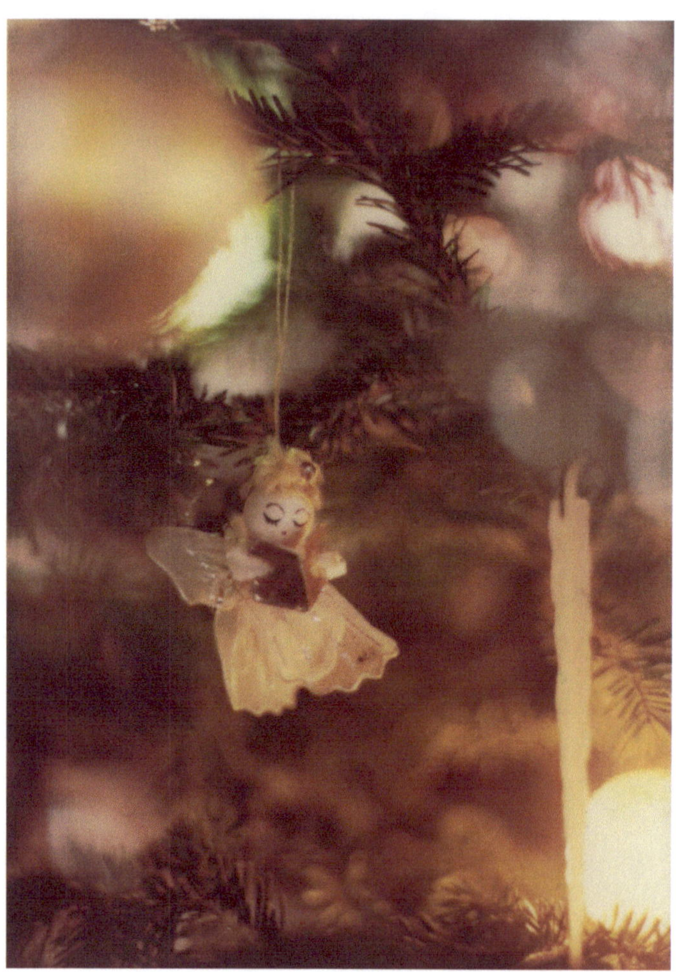

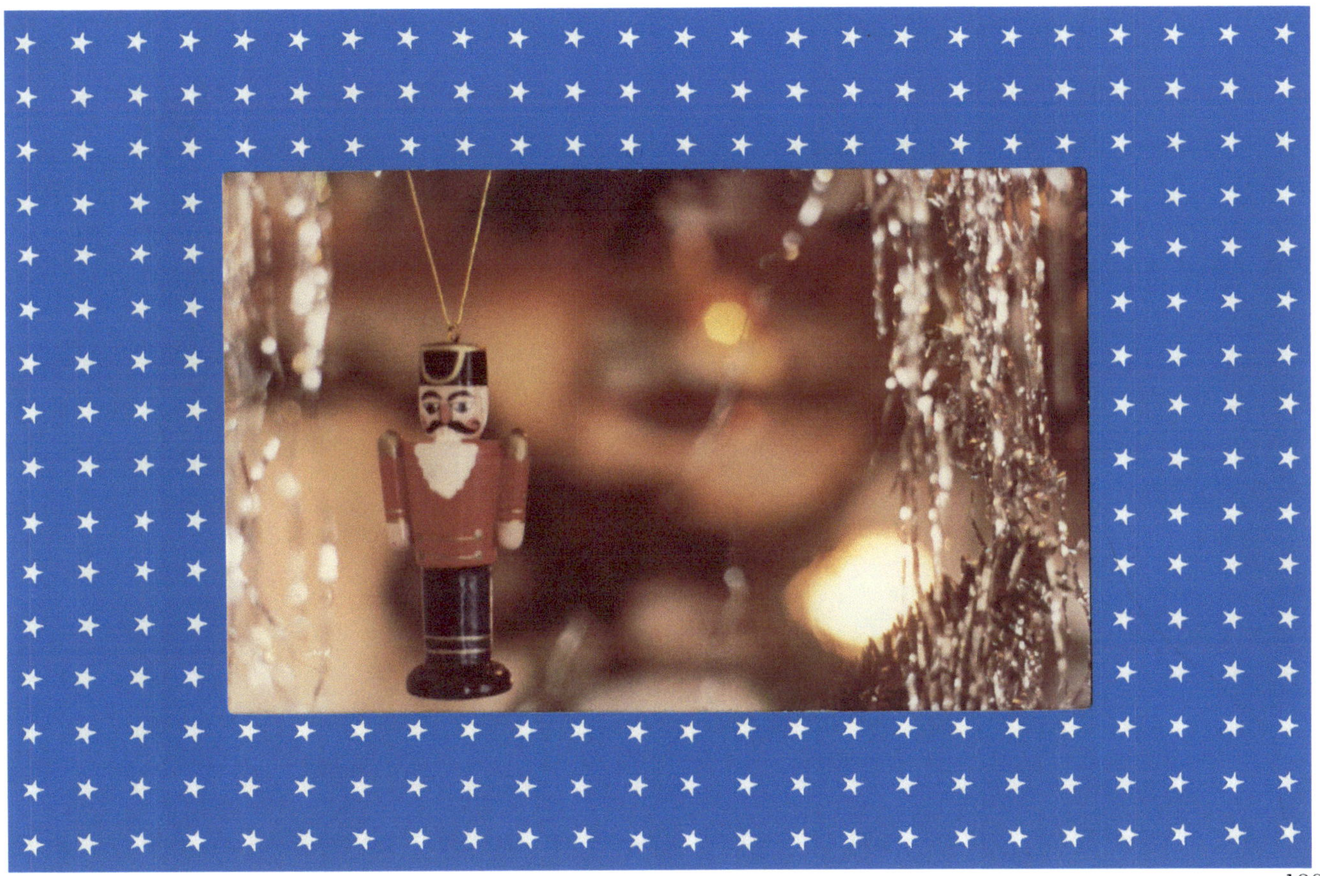

1982

# Playing Santa

2005

He bought the red suit in July. Figured no one would realize what he was doing. Secretly worked on the trim late at night, after everyone else had gone to bed.

The weight: he'd been adding to that for as long as he could remember.

The beard was tough. He'd actually started several times, but it was never white enough, or it itched too much, or someone demanded it be cut back. In the end, he had to use one of his wishes, and that made it fluffy and white and, oddly enough, pleased the genie immensely.

Boots, belt, gloves, those were all easy to find after Halloween had gone (which was a relief, because of all the ghosts — not the Christmas ghosts, those lesson bearers and morality players, but the *other* kind).

From the beginning, he knew he'd have to use one of his wishes on the reindeer. He asked for nine — one with a red nose — all able to fly and pull his sleigh, which he'd built himself, down to the last bell.

(Building the sleigh was easy because the garage was *his* playground, off limits to the rest of the family.)

When Christmas Eve arrived, the genie emerged from the lamp and said, "Remember, you've only got one wish left."

"I know," said the man, but he was grinning, and this seemed to make the genie rather nervous. "I wish to be able to grant one wish to every child on earth."

The genie did some quick calculations and shook his head. "That would be more than six billion wishes. You've only got one."

He knew better than to argue with a genie, and despaired.

"However," the genie said, "I'm not unreasonable, so this is what I'll do: fly your sleigh to a spot, it doesn't matter where, so people — a lot of people — can see you, and I'll give you a sack that will not empty of presents until dawn's first light."

This is where the story falls apart, as the reindeer took this Santa and his sleigh *somewhere...*

Maybe you've seen him?

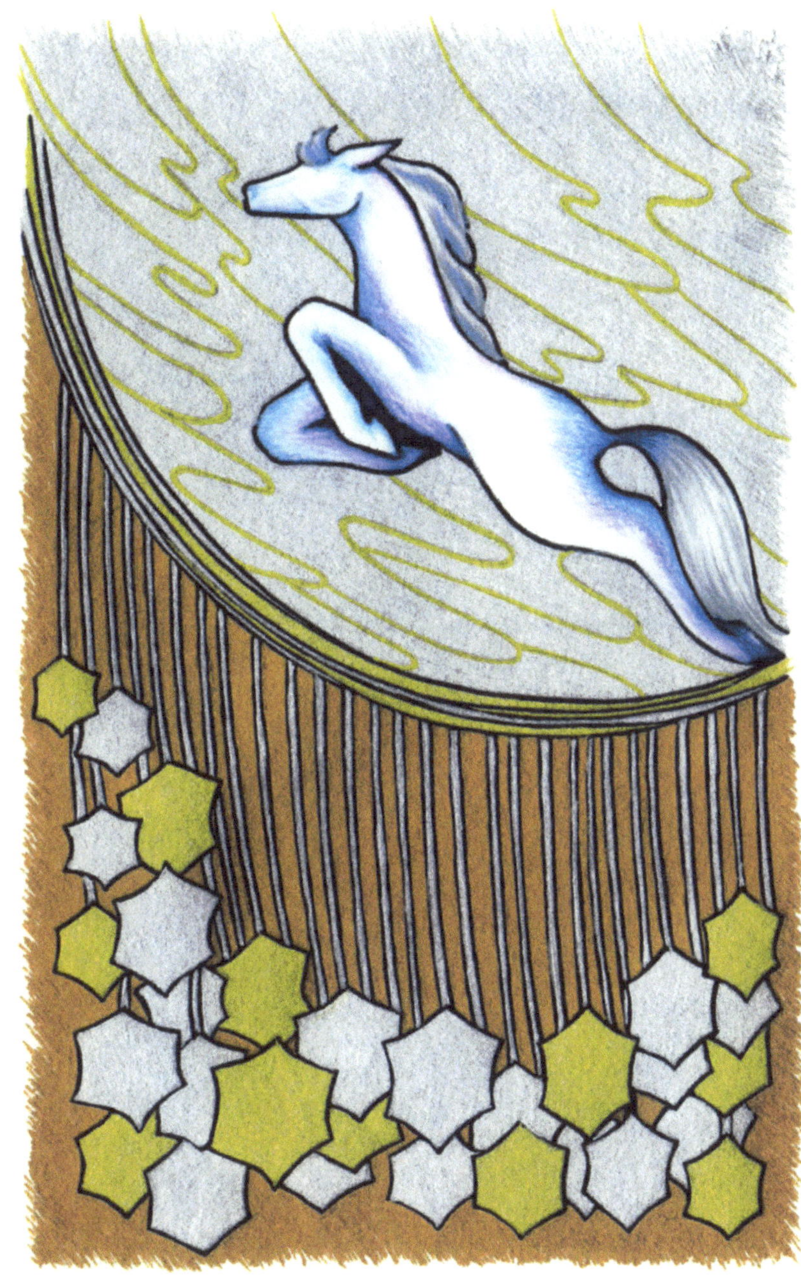

2011

# Flight of the Snowflake

2006

The snowflakes have a belief, though they don't often speak of it. South, they say, life is more exciting, albeit shorter. And it's true, Southern Hemisphere snowflakes say the same about life in the north.

Of course, most snowflakes want a long, comfortable life, and eschew excitement in all its forms. That's why you find so many in the vast, snowy metropolises of Nova Scotia and Greenland and Siberia. Some of the oldest snowflakes, in fact, gather crowds numbering in the millions to tell their stories of the good old days, often to do with ice ages or Neanderthals or great woolly mammoths.

It's true these older snowflakes are often so ancient, they're dusty (if you've never seen a dusty snowflake, then the snow you've seen is young). But their lives, hundreds of thousands of days, can be recapped quite simply. They stay where they are, they see nothing new, they hear nothing but the wind, they do nothing whatsoever. Their life stories become repetitious.

Which may be why so many younger snowflakes crave excitement. Adventure. Yes, even danger. The life of a snowflake starts with a fall—sometimes gentle, sometimes a blizzard—but after that it's mostly sitting around until they melt. Sure, some end up in snowball fights, and that can be tremendous fun. But they can just as easily end up on the butt of a snowman. It's really not up to them.

Not usually.

Sally Snowflake hitched a ride south one December night, tucked away on the back of a sleigh. She was old, yes, but her heart was young, and she yearned for thrills, however brief.

She ditched the sleigh somewhere near Miami, where an unusual cold spell was insufficient to keep her alive. Sally Snowflake cried as she melted, but trust me, they were joyous tears. Her journey had been swift and bumpy, and she saw half a continent—more than even the most frantic nor'easter snowflakes ever saw.

Funny thing, about the final moments of a snowflake's life; they're more akin to that of a caterpillar, which is reborn as a butterfly. Last I heard, Sally Snowflake was still drifting along the Caribbean with all the other drops of rain that make up the seas.

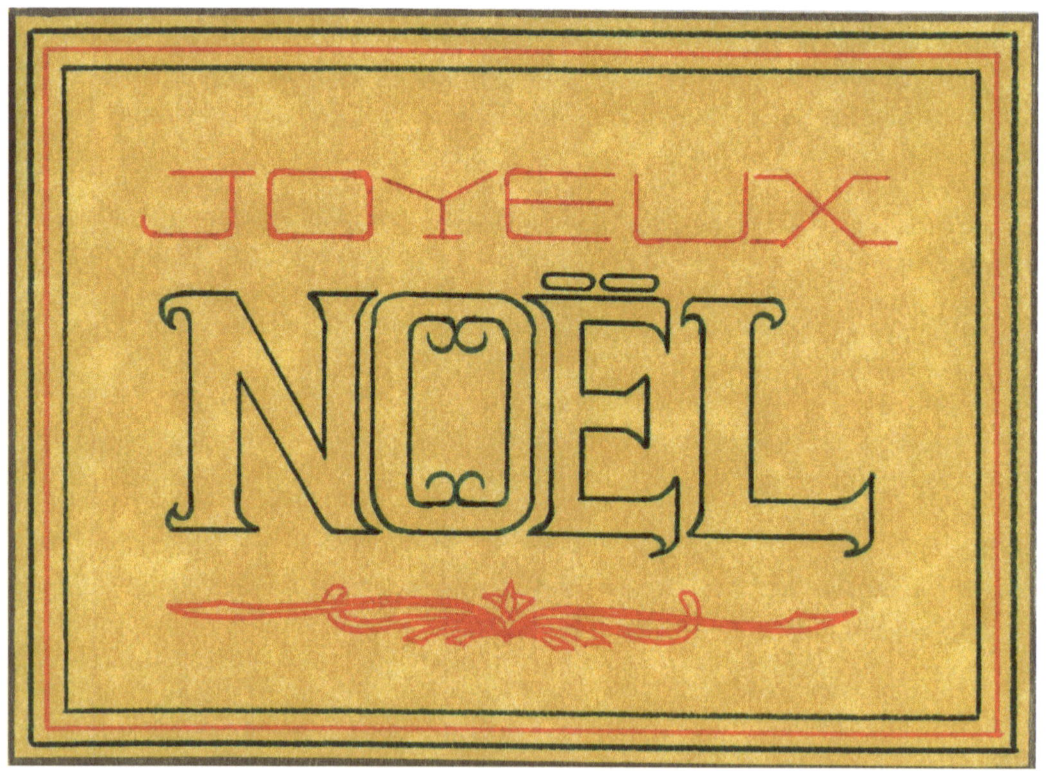
JOYEUX
NOËL

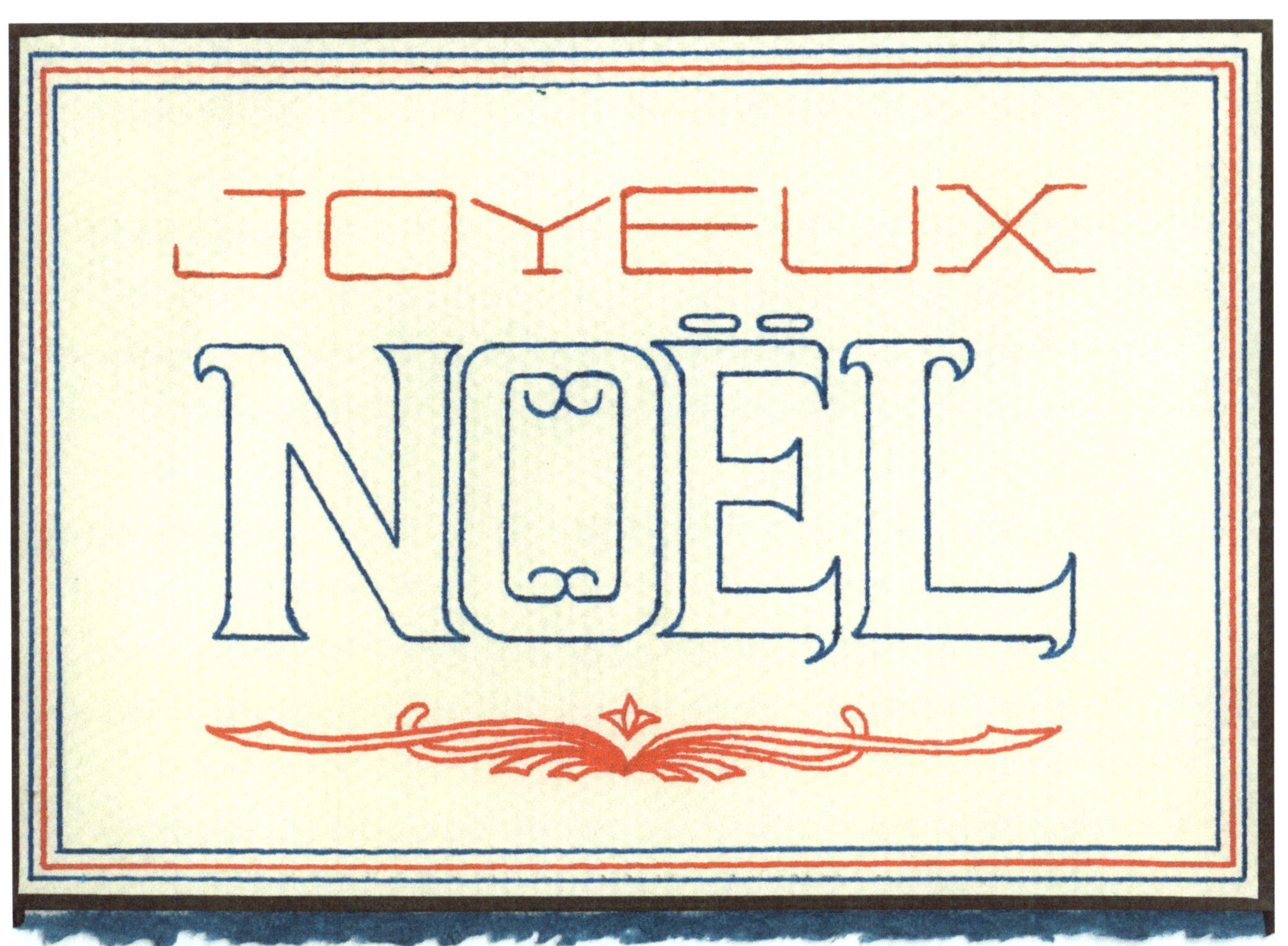


1997

# The Sylvester Bros. Traveling Christmas Show & Extravaganza

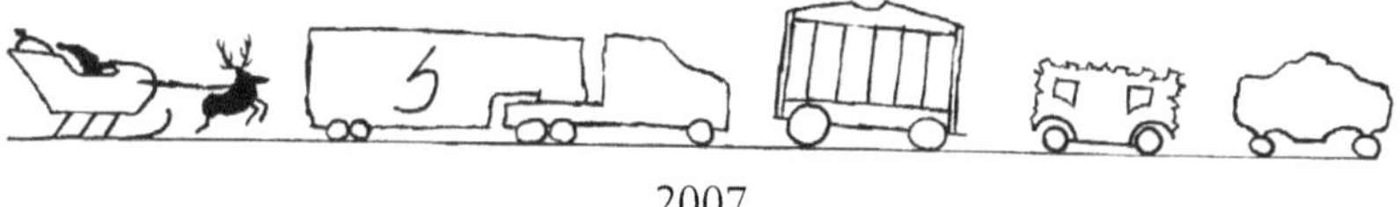

2007

One of the Sylvester brothers is dead. Has been for a long number of years. This doesn't stop him from traveling with the Christmas troupe, mind you. If you've seen the show, you probably thought he was a Marley impersonator. (Rumors suggest he is, in fact, more than just friends with one of the ghosts of Christmas Past.)

It's a one-ring, one-tent show. Make no mistake, you don't arrive at the Sylvester Bros. Traveling Christmas Show & Extravaganza expecting spectacle. You probably expect, at best, something cute. Carolers. Eggnog vendors and aluminum pickles for your trees.

The candles and clay dreidels probably surprise you. ("A great miracle happened here," proclaim the toys.)

A juggling chipmunk sits on the back of a reindeer called Prancer while she trots around the ring.

There's a woman from Somalia telling stories about The Seven Principles of Kwanzaa, but she does it in Swahili. (Kwanzaa, by the way, translates to "first fruits.")

Icelandic songs welcome winter.

They have drummers, pipers, lords-a-leaping, and ladies-dancing.

Saint Stephen, in his laurel crown, will regale you with hilarious tales of Saint Nicholas as a child.

Fruit cakes are available. And the mistletoe is fresh.

At the Sylvester Bros. Traveling Christmas Show & Extravaganza, there is no such thing as a War on Christmas. Indeed, they celebrate every day anyone anywhere in the world celebrates Christmas, including all Twelve Days.

Kris Kringle, Father Christmas (astride a goat), and the original Coca-Cola Santa all get a chance to take a bow. Don't miss Neclaus' tales about the Laughing Valley of Hohaho. If you're interested, someone will guide you through the nativity, with the shepherds, the wise men (and they may present you with gifts of gold, frankincense, or myrrh), the Star of Bethlehem, and of course the babe wrapped in swaddling clothes.

The show never stops. Day and night, on it goes, until they strike the tent, load up the sleighs (and trucks), and set off for the next location, wherever that may be.

The only day The Sylvester Bros. Traveling Christmas Show & Extravaganza does not perform is Boxing Day. If you show up, they'll feed you ham and crumpets and, if you believe the stories, they may offer to let you open the box. You should remember to ask the wren (yes, the king of birds himself) for a good harvest.

Should you meet the living Sylvester brother, be sure to thank him profusely, and leave gifts, lest he opt not to bring his troupe again in your direction.

Whatever you expect, you'll undoubtedly find at the Sylvester Bros. Traveling Christmas Show & Extravaganza. So when you go, expect miracles.

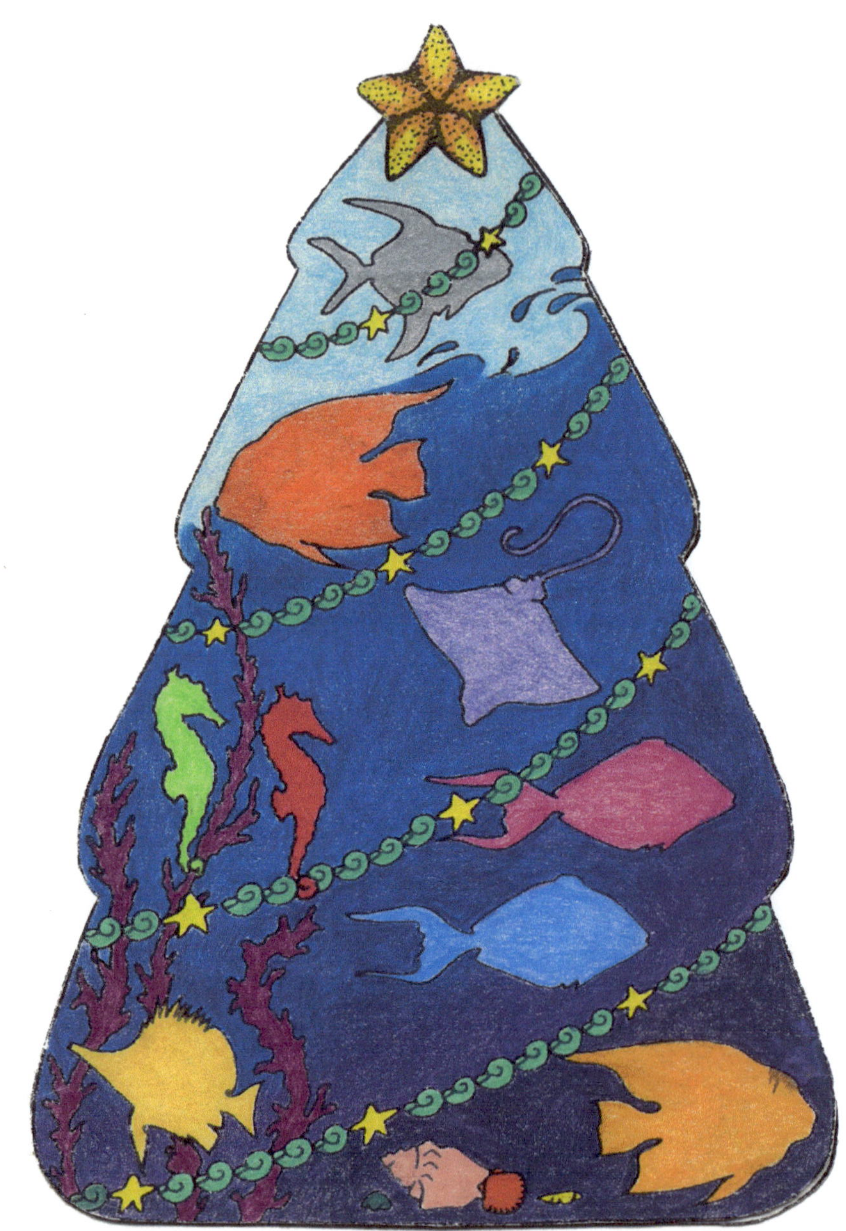

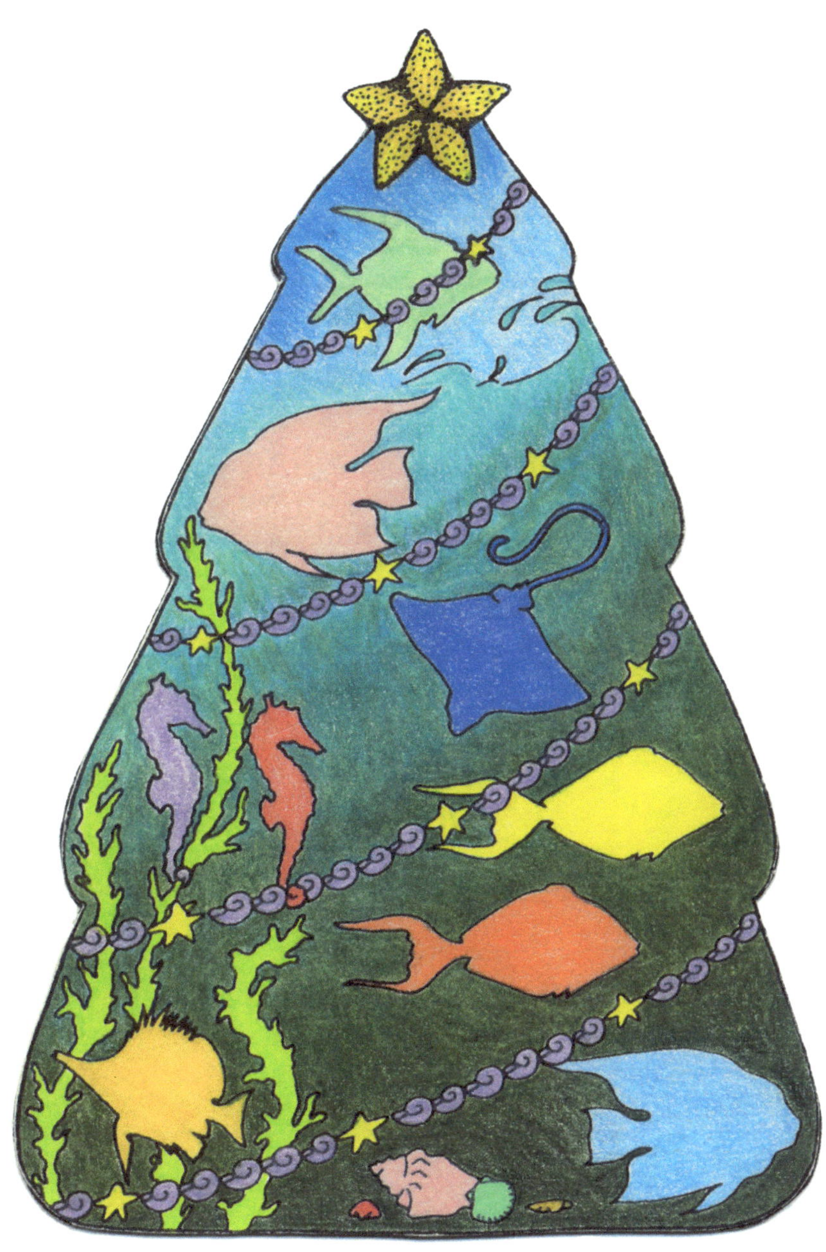

1990

# The Forgotten Mailbox

2008

Once upon a time, perhaps, it was a thriving neighborhood, with bakers and bankers and businessmen, gangs of happy children, ice cream trucks, and sparkling dreams. But that was long ago. Now, it is mostly abandoned, and those who stay only stay for a brief time. They go either to better or worse places.

There's a phone booth which hasn't had a dial tone since the 70's. There's an old car that's melted into the street and seems to float on cracked asphalt like an iceberg. There's a mailbox which has not been on any postman's route for as long as the postmaster himself has been alive.

And there's a girl—we'll call her Sue—who writes a simple letter to Santa. Sue's a quiet girl, and has moved with her parents so frequently she barely knows her own name.

The letter says:

> Dear Santa,
>
> Please send me a doll and a friend.

When she goes to drop it in the box, there's a boy—we'll call him Joe. "Ain't nobody ever sends letters through that box no more," he says.

"Why not?"

"No one to pick 'em up. No one to deliver 'em. So no one ever gets what you send."

"Some things get sent no matter who picks them up," she tells him, showing that the letter is addressed to Santa at the North Pole.

"That's all fun and games," Joe says, "but that's more a rustbox than a postbox anymore, and no one's gonna get your letter, not even the Big Guy himself. Anyway, look around you, we're right at the heart of nowhere. No one comes here who ain't lost."

"I'm not lost," she tells him.

"And anyways," Joe adds, "Christmas is tomorrow." You wouldn't know it, not there, as no lights decorate the street, no tinsel hangs from any tree, and no trees have made it into the cramped little apartment holes.

"He'll get it," Sue stubbornly says. "And he'll come." The mailbox doesn't open easily, or soundlessly, but it opens, and she drops the unstamped envelope into the mailbox.

Next day, bright and early–because even in a place where dreams seem as forgotten as a rusty old abandoned mailbox, children rise early–Sue rushes to the street corner. Her parents had given her something small and practical, like socks, and something for each other—and one of those things is a seed of hope though they don't yet know it. Sue rushes to the box thinking perhaps something might've been left for here there.

She finds Joe.

"Morning," he says, grinning. It's the way he's always grinned, in all the hours she's known him.

"Morning."

"So, did the Big Guy come?" Joe asks.

"I got socks," she tells him.

"I got underwear."

"That's useful," she says.

"Very."

"Anything else?" she asks.

He shakes his head. Sue frowns, because socks are nothing like a doll. She climbs onto her tiptoes and opens the squeaky mailbox, but the slot is too narrow and the insides too dark. She sees nothing.

"I'm sorry," Joe says. "I know I said he wouldn't come, and he didn't, but I really wish he did."

She lets the box slam shut, and the bottom half—the locked bit, from which the postmen of old would've collected the mail—that bottom half swings open a mere quarter inch. It's enough to stop Joe. It's enough to pique their interest. It's enough to make Sue open the forgotten mailbox.

The shadows inside are deep, and drip like syrup, and it's hard to see through the gloom and the spider webs and the dry, cough-filled air. The dust finally settles to reveal two bright packages. One's green, and labeled Joe. The red one says Sue.

Joe opens his present. It's an old book, in fair condition, its spine crinkled but the title and author clear. If this was Joe's story, you'd understand why it wets his eyes with tears, and why he'll treasure that paperback for the rest of his life.

Sue opens hers. It's a doll. She doesn't know it yet, but it's just like the doll her mom had when she was Sue's age, and it may in fact be the very same doll. But it's a smiling doll, and a smiling Sue, and a smiling if tearful Joe.

With great care and no small bit of reverence, Sue closes the mailbox door, and checks to see that it's locked itself once again. She whispers so that only the forgotten mailbox can hear, and says, "Thank you."

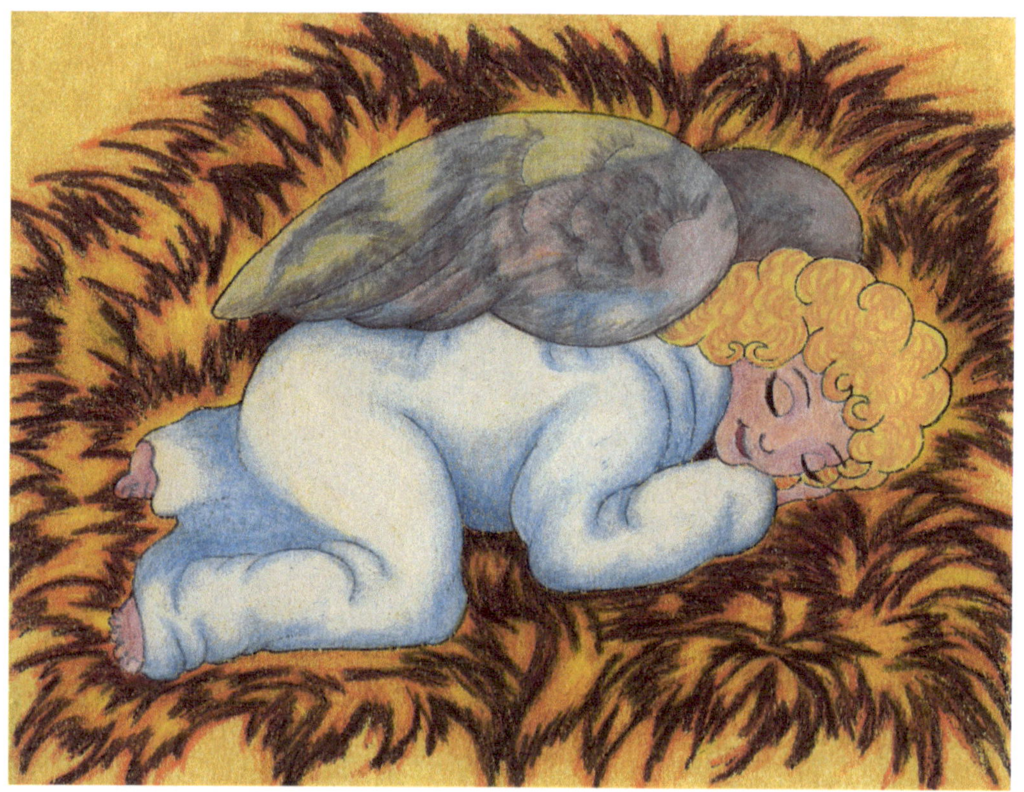

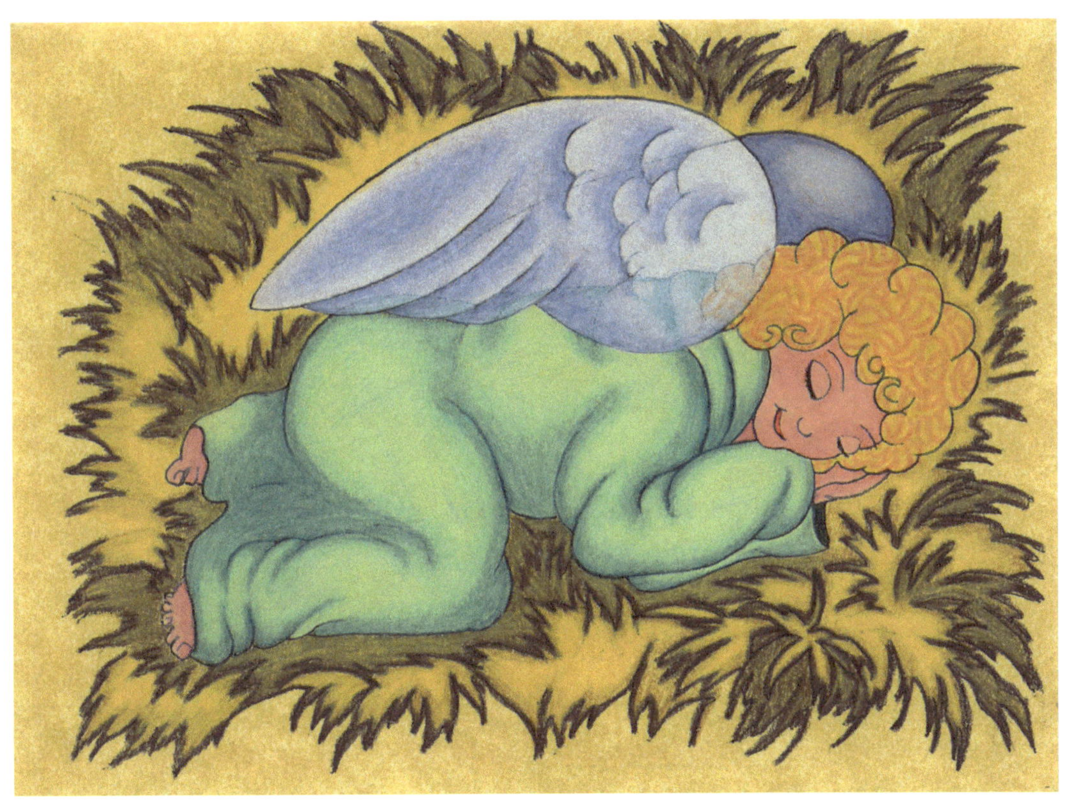

1992

# Snow Flakes

2009

One snowflake said to another, "I call dibs on that house."

And indeed, it was a marvelous house, the perfect size, with exactly the right amount of lawn and porch and roof, and not a single speck of snow resting upon it. Smoke drifted from the chimney, children laughed and played inside, someone sipped hot chocolate. A snowflake can sense all these things, can hear the songs and wishes, sometimes even the prayers when it's appropriate for a snowflake to hear.

The other snowflake said, "But I want that one." And then it dove.

Snowflakes love to drift. They love to float and flutter and flit. They're pre-eminent dancers, from whom mankind originally learned rhythm. (Yes, of course, there are raindrops who insist they were more responsible, but this time of year, no one takes the raindrops seriously.) Snowflakes don't generally move with all that much speed.

The first snowflake, determined to make that house its own, also dove, and the race was on.

Snowflakes, generally, don't gather in large audience to watch a race, and rarely do they support a favorite. Rather, they join the fray, they jostle for the first spot, they get caught up in the furious flurry. Only one can win. Only one can claim being first on that perfect house with its perfect inhabitants.

The winner reached the chimney first. First is important. First makes the house yours, if you're a snowflake.

The snowflake danced and jigged and laughed at its brothers and sisters, but they couldn't stop. By the dozen, the hundred, the thousand, other snowflakes fell upon the rooftop, the porch, the lawn, and the two who had begun the race.

"Ah, well," the first snowflake said, as though such words were not inevitable, "there's plenty of room for all!"

Later in the night, as the perfect home-dwellers slept in their perfect rooms, while even the first two snowflakes rested peacefully, when nothing could be seen of the lawn or the porch or the rooftop but a white blanket of snow, another snowflake, falling high above, said to another, "I want that house."

"It's a good house," the other snowflake agreed. "It is getting rather crowded, though."

"That's okay. There's plenty of room." They joined the piles, the drifts, and the heaps.

By dawn, Christmas morning, a million snowflakes, united in sparkling celebration, had settled quite comfortably and, mostly, fallen into slumber.

Before running downstairs to see what Santa might've brought, the children pressed their faces to their bedroom windows, and one said, quite smugly, "I told you Santa would bring us a white Christmas."

Atop the chimney, two of the one million snowflakes giggled quietly.

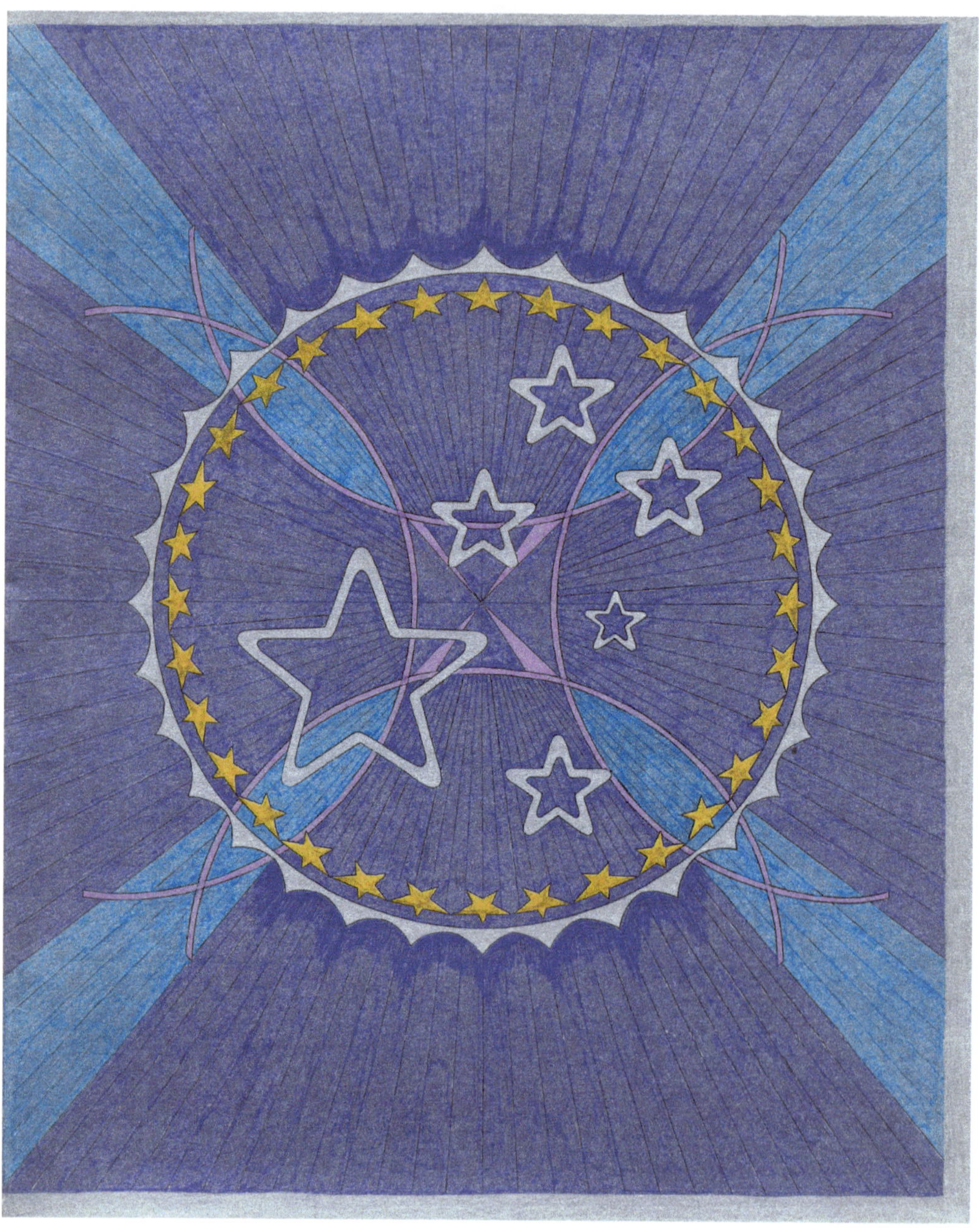

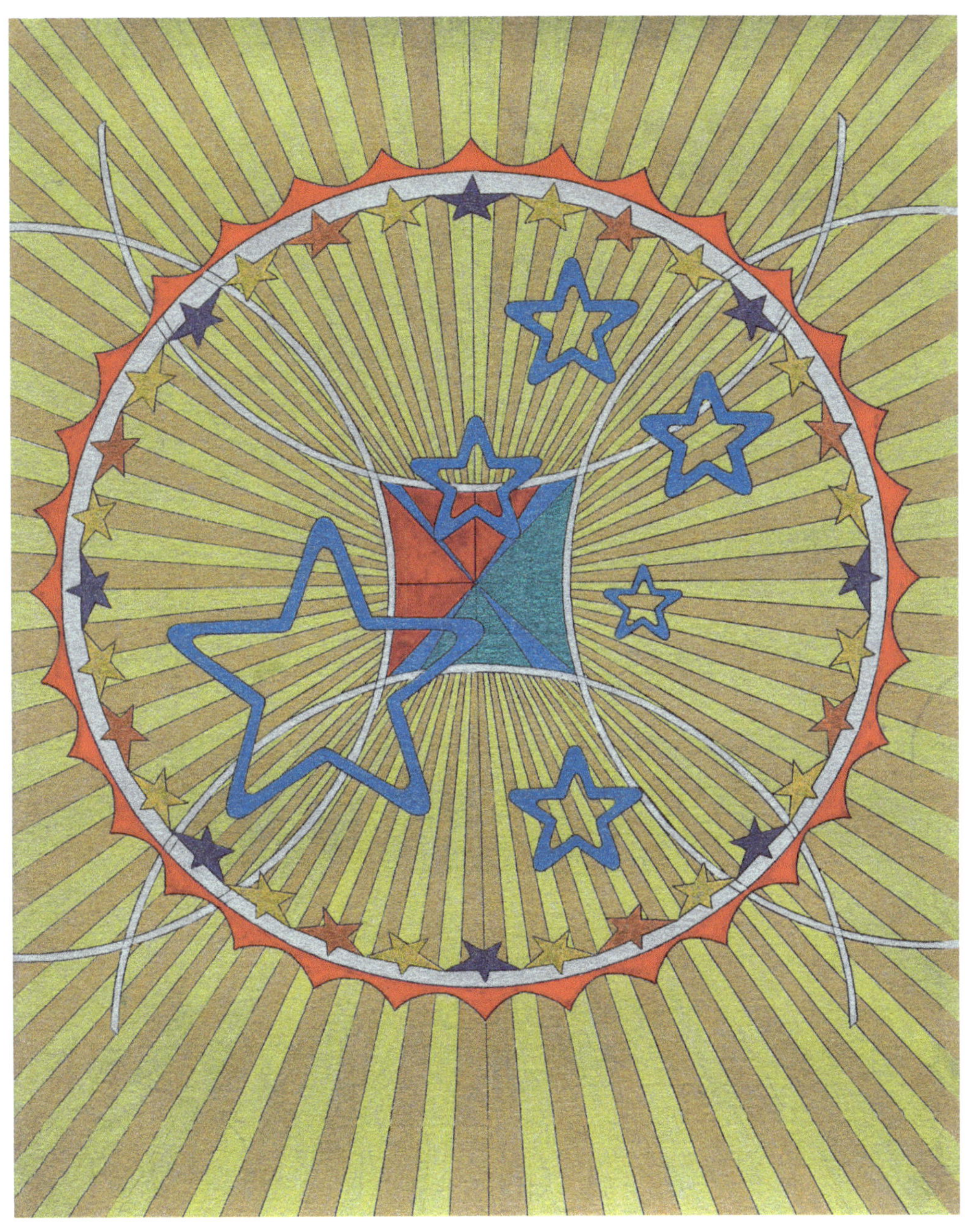

2004

# Old Man Winter

2010

'Twas the night, yes, before Christmas, and I invited Old Man Winter into my home. He gratefully accepted a mug of hot chocolate with marshmallows, took off his wool gloves, and sat by the fireplace.

Though old, as his name implied, he was strong and alert. He talked about this year's Harvest Feast. He likes pumpkin soup. I do not. We talked about snowstorms in December. He laughed and said that, in June and July, he often visits Chile and Australia and New Zealand.

"I don't bring the cold," he confided. "I merely witness it."

We talked about hockey and snow angels, icicles, sleighs, and the moral implications of using coal as eyes. He claimed to have climbed Kilimanjaro, twice, to touch the equatorial glaciers. He told me about the winter carnivals that no longer circled the globe, their trapeze artists flying through the air, the polar bears, the juggling clowns in blue and silver suits.

After finishing his hot chocolate he pulled his gloves back on, threw on his long winter coat, and said, "There's much to do tonight. Much to witness."

I watched from my apartment window as he walked down the street, but I'm not so sure I actually saw what I saw. He reached the last building on the road, looked around once, then bounded up the side, window ledge to window ledge, utilizing crevices I couldn't see in the bricks. On the rooftop, he cast out a net and captured the bitingly cold wind, all of the wind, until the air was still. He folded the net down, folding again and again until it was small enough to fit into his pocket, then looked back at me and winked.

Old Man Winter said, and I'm quite sure I heard him as though he stood beside me whispering, "Hope the holiday season warms your heart, my friend."

And then he was gone.

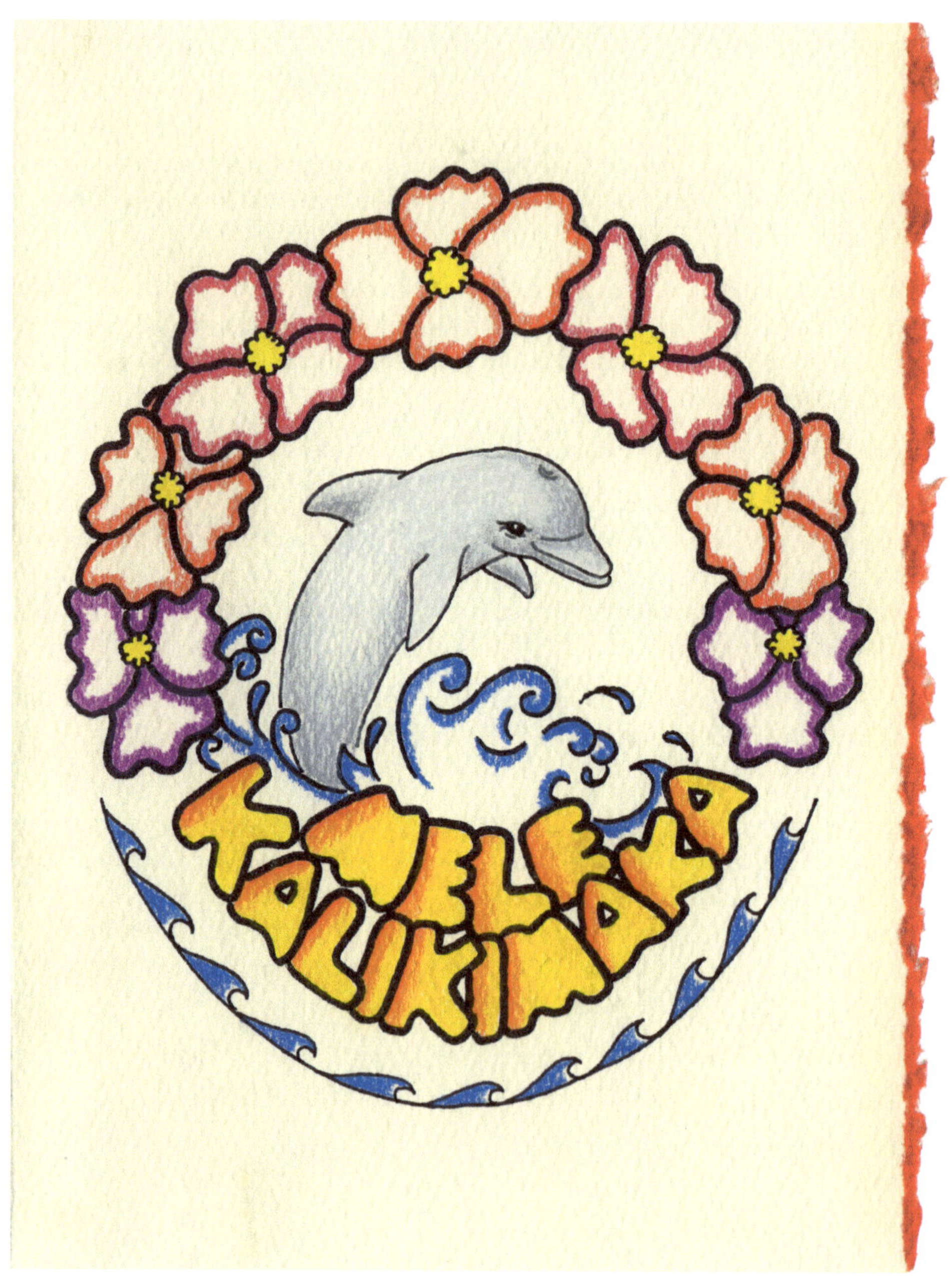
MELE
KALIKIMAKA

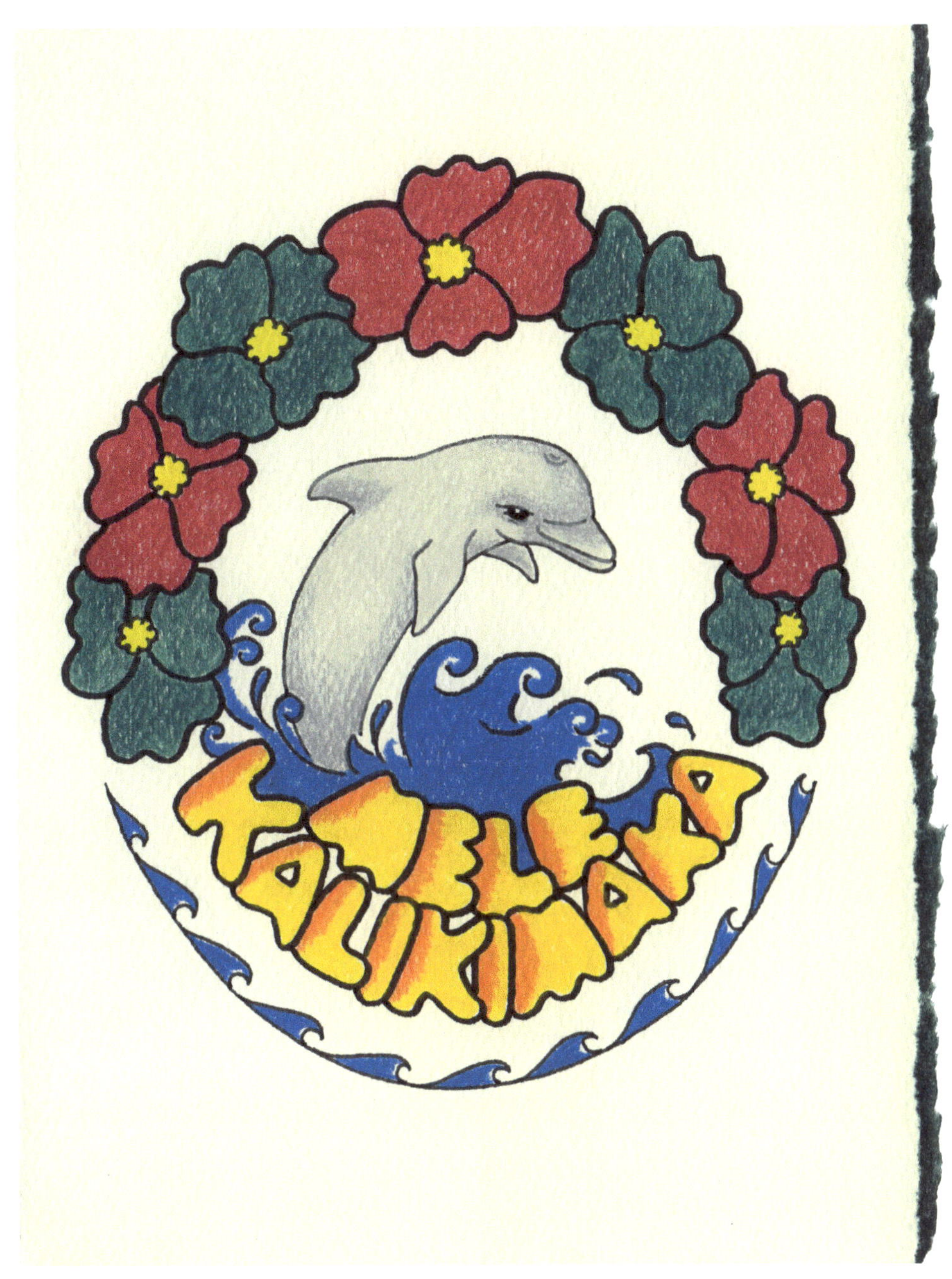

1999

# A Southern Breeze

2011

The life of a southern breeze is usually pretty easy. You pick up a bit of heat off the coast of Guatemala, you take a leisurely spin underneath the Florida Keys, maybe stop for a forbidden dance in Cuba or some Bahamian spiced rum. You caress bathing beauties, tussle hair, catch a sail, and maybe grow up to be something big, something named.

But sometimes, perhaps when the northern winds seem a little more brisk, when the east winds whistle nonchalantly across busy, shopper-filled avenues, a southern breeze gets an idea.

This one unnamed southern breeze, late in December, decided it had had enough of Miami and Mexico City and Martinique. No, this little breeze thought a trip to New York, to see the tree at Rockefeller Center, would be a good idea.

The other breezes laughed and scoffed and teased. You couldn't be a southern breeze so far north of the Mason-Dixon Line. This time of year, you couldn't even get that far. But this southern breeze was determined.

As far north as Savannah, where its sultry cousins warned against going further, the southern breeze had a gentle time of it. Soon after, however, the going got rough. Other winds, unrelated, got in the way. They weren't mean about it; they just didn't have time, busy as they were blowing this way or that.

The southern breeze pushed forward with all its might, through the Carolinas, and even Virginia, before reaching the tumultuous hot air over Washington D.C. There, the journey might have ended—for some other breeze. Not this southern breeze. With a great deal of effort, the breeze found Maryland, and Delaware, and Jersey.

By now, the southern breeze was cold. Shivering. Freezing, even. But it continued, persistent, finally crossing the Hudson River and entering Manhattan. The streets confused it. The subways sent up breezes of their own, breezes that spoke too quickly and too brusquely. No one offered to help.

Alone, the little southern breeze made it to Central Park, and played a while around the ice skating rink. Then, it found Rockefeller Center, and the great big brilliantly lit-up tree, and all sorts of bundled-up people around it. The breeze rustled the tree's limbs and danced amid the lights, and there, in the dark of Christmas Eve, in that seventy-something foot spruce, the little southern breeze settled for a long nap filled with warm dreams.

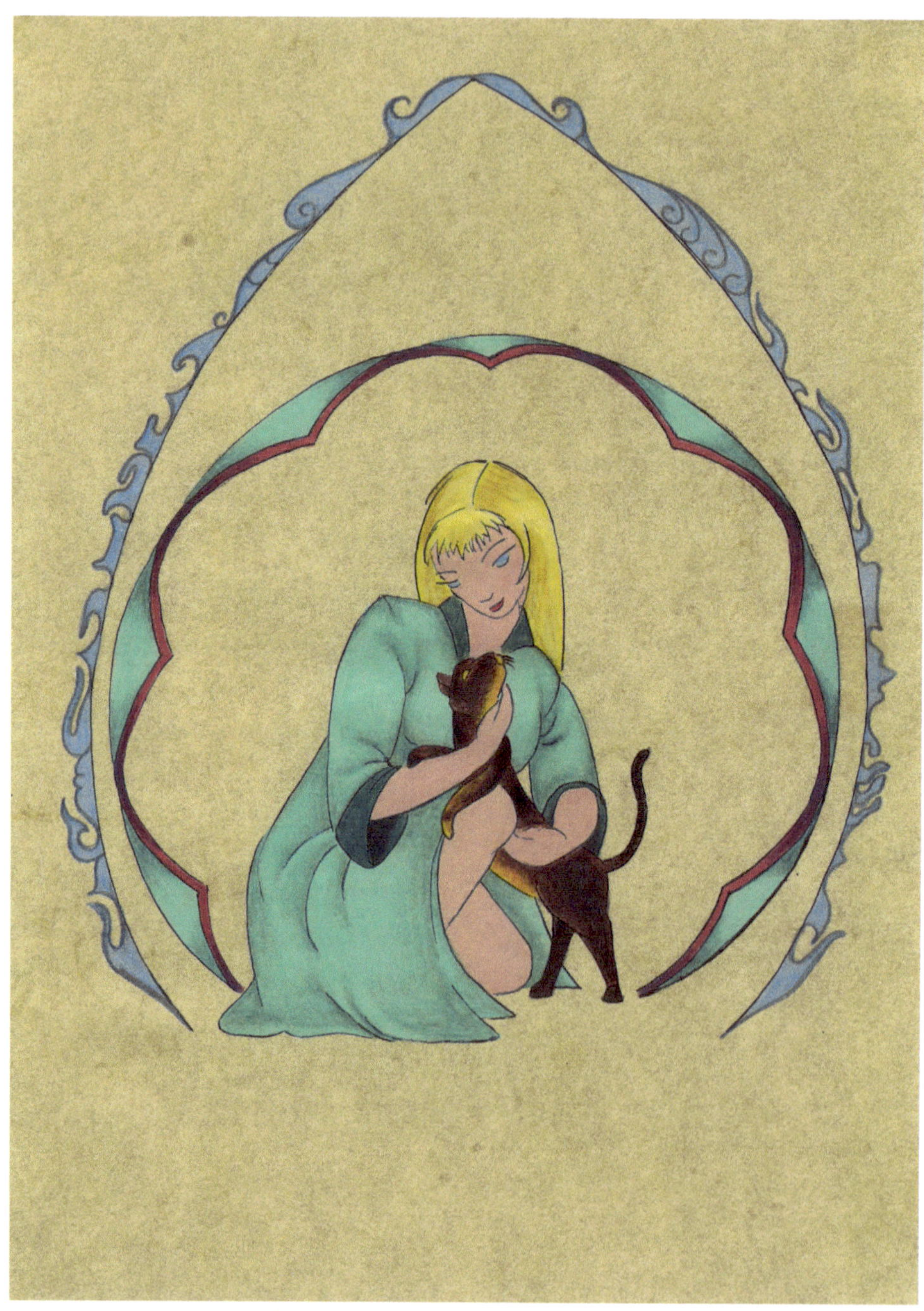

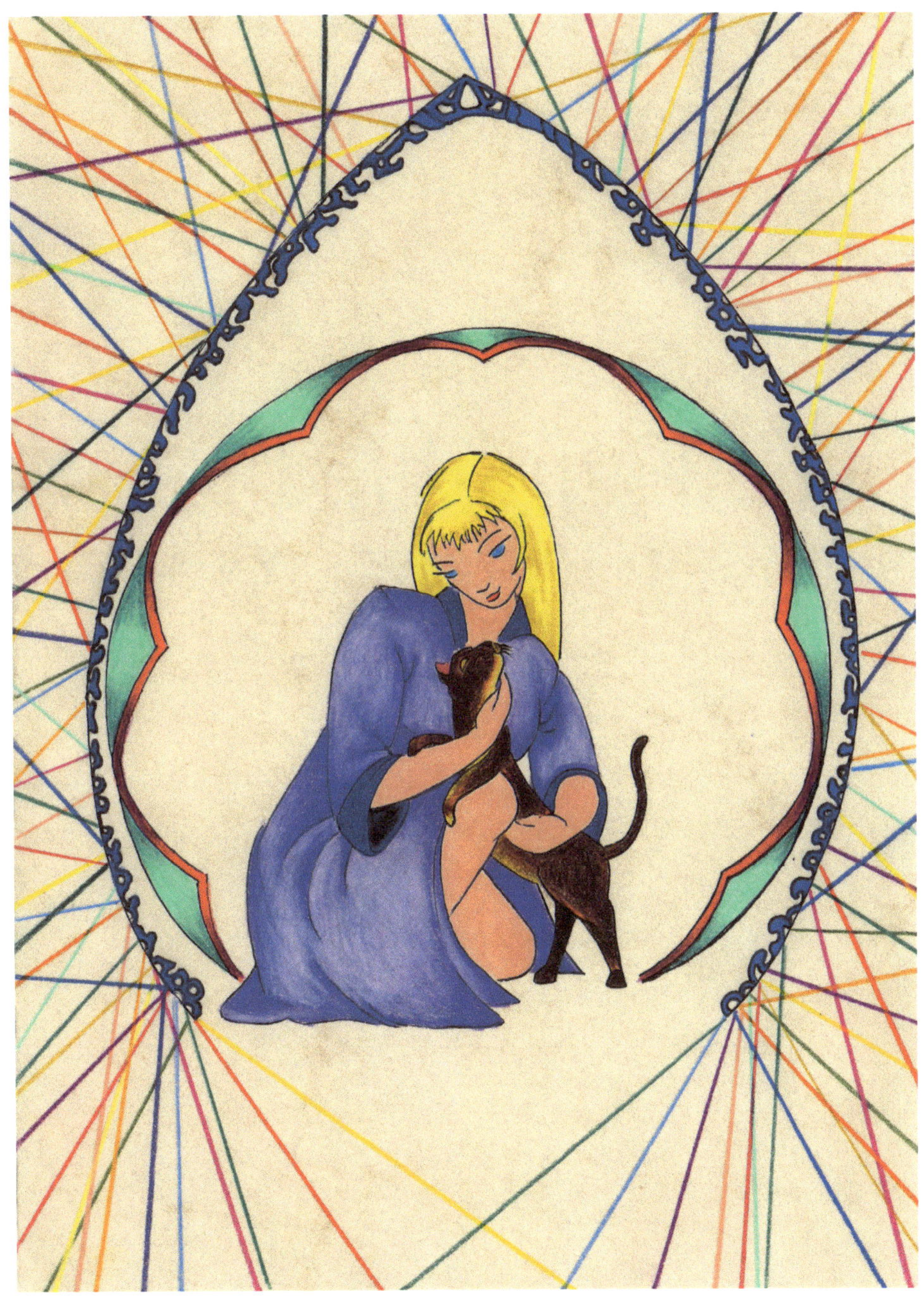

1995

# The Unfulfilled Fairy

2012

While it may be generally believed that a fairy's life is filled with luscious green forests, crazy light shows, unmapped roads, and magical shenanigans, and that such a life may be enough for most magically born creatures, this one fairy, whom we'll call Bob, found it to be unfulfilling and insufficient. Bob the fairy said, to all who would listen, "I'd much rather be an angel."

"But you can't be an angel," said Bob the fairy's mother, also, quite naturally, a fairy. "You have fairy wings, which are very much like butterfly wings. Beautiful and awe inspiring as they may be, fairy wings are not, and do not ever resemble, angel wings. Fairy wings cannot take you so high as an angel's wings must be able to take an angel."

"Still," Bob the fairy said, "I'd much rather be an angel."

"But you can't be an angel," said Bob the fairy's human servant, who was pretty and, once upon a time, had found herself lost in a woodland. "You have a fairy's natural inclination toward mischief and alcohol, and angels, as you know, do not drink wine. And angels, as you know, do not play humans for fools."

"Still," Bob the fairy said, "I'd much rather be an angel."

"But you can't be an angel," said Bob the fairy's friend Francesca. "That's just foolish."

So Bob the fairy examined his wings quite closely in a mirror, and knew his mother spoke the truth. Then Bob the fairy released his human servant, a full four years before fulfilling her contract—albeit, he never guided her back home. And finally, Bob the fairy had to concede Francesca was the wiser.

After all this thought and consideration, Bob the fairy said, "If I cannot be an angel, then perhaps I can be an elf." He travelled north, far north, into snowy icy realms, seeking an elven colony of which he'd heard tell, and he found the elves. Bob the fairy presented himself. He said, "Hello, elves. I am Bob the fairy, and though I'd much rather be an angel, I believe it would be just as brilliant to be an elf."

The big man in charge, jolly and red-cheeked, gave Bob the fairy a thorough looking-over and admitted, "I can always use another good toymaker. Welcome aboard."

And that is how Bob the fairy became the first fairy of Christmastown.

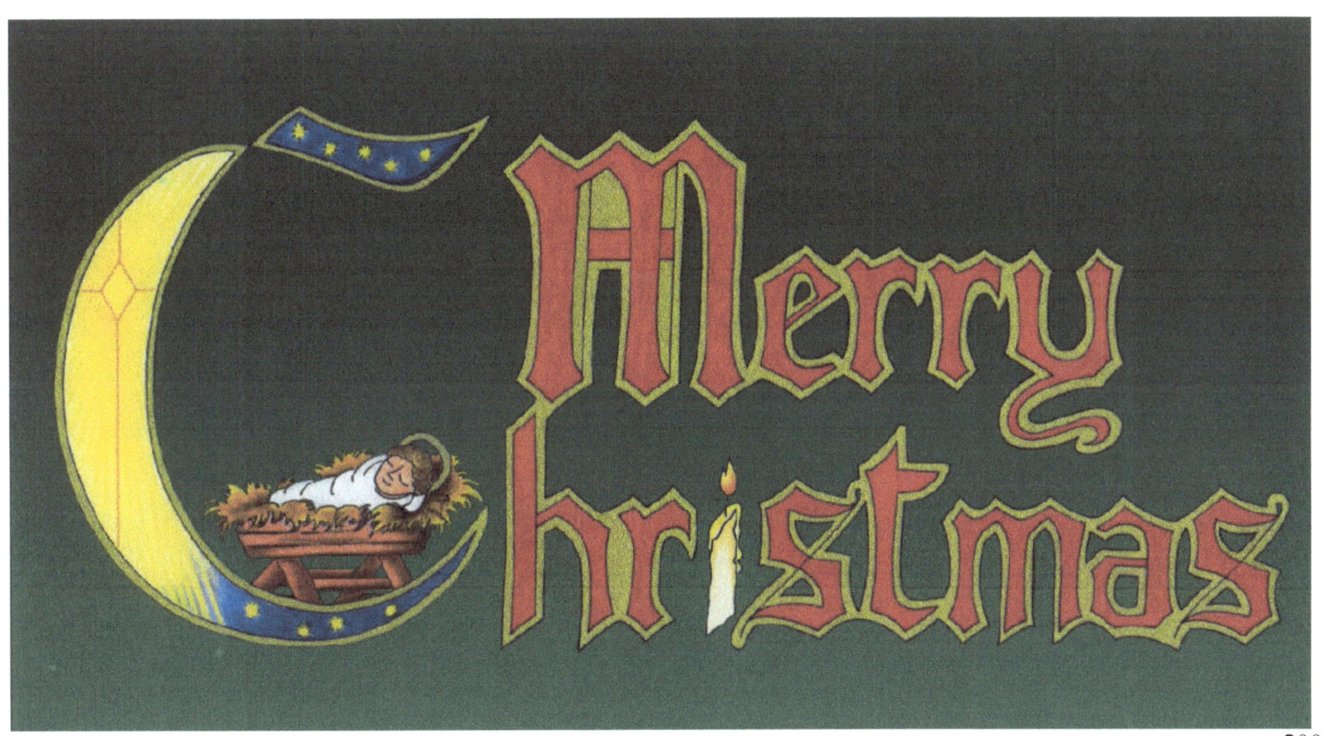


2008

# Operation: North Pole

2013

When the northern lights hit the spires of ice, they burst with color and the tinkling of bells. The city stands tall and deep, carved out of ice and snow, shrouded half a year in the dark of night.

It's an ancient city. The scents of roasting and baking still waft through its streets. The air itself tastes of candy canes and nutmeg.

But the city is empty. Deserted. Abandoned long ago. The colonel frowns as she flips through reports in the middle of what they've dubbed Main Street. The scientists are having their own special sort of Christmas, making discoveries and observations and theories. But this isn't what they were seeking.

It's the third such city in ice, the third indication of civilization predating the Egyptians and the Chinese, and the third disappointment of the season.

A voice crackled on her radio. "Sir," the voice says. "We've found something."

In an icy basement of an icy structure, the Colonel joins a pair of her explorer soldiers and one of the scientists. The scientist holds something at the end of a long-limbed set of tweezers. Unlike anything else in this frozen city, it is neither ice nor snow. And it's not twelve thousand years old.

It's a shred of gift label. Red. Sparkly. With the name of a recipient on the inside.

"Amazing," the scientist says.

The Colonel barely acknowledges the comment. Of course it's amazing. It's unexpected, unwarranted, unheard of. And though it doesn't say Colonel on the gift tag, it is most certainly the Colonel's name.

"That's it," she says. "Pack up. We're done." When they look questioningly at her, she says, "We're not going to find what we're looking for here."

The scientists resist, of course, but they'll return with full teams and all the proper equipment to map out every corner of the ice city. Within three hours, the helicopters are lifting off the ice and headed south.

The Colonel stares wistfully from the helicopter as they fly away.

She doesn't see that her team has been seen. She doesn't see the elf lowering his binoculars and picking up his satellite phone. He dials the switchboard in Copenhagen and says, "They're leaving."

There's a delay before the response. "Again. They'll be back. We'll inform the big guy."

The switchboard in Copenhagen sends the message to seventeen regional offices across the world. The big guy is at one of them – or about to arrive. It's been a long time since the workshop could operate efficiently from a single remote location deep in the Arctic Circle.

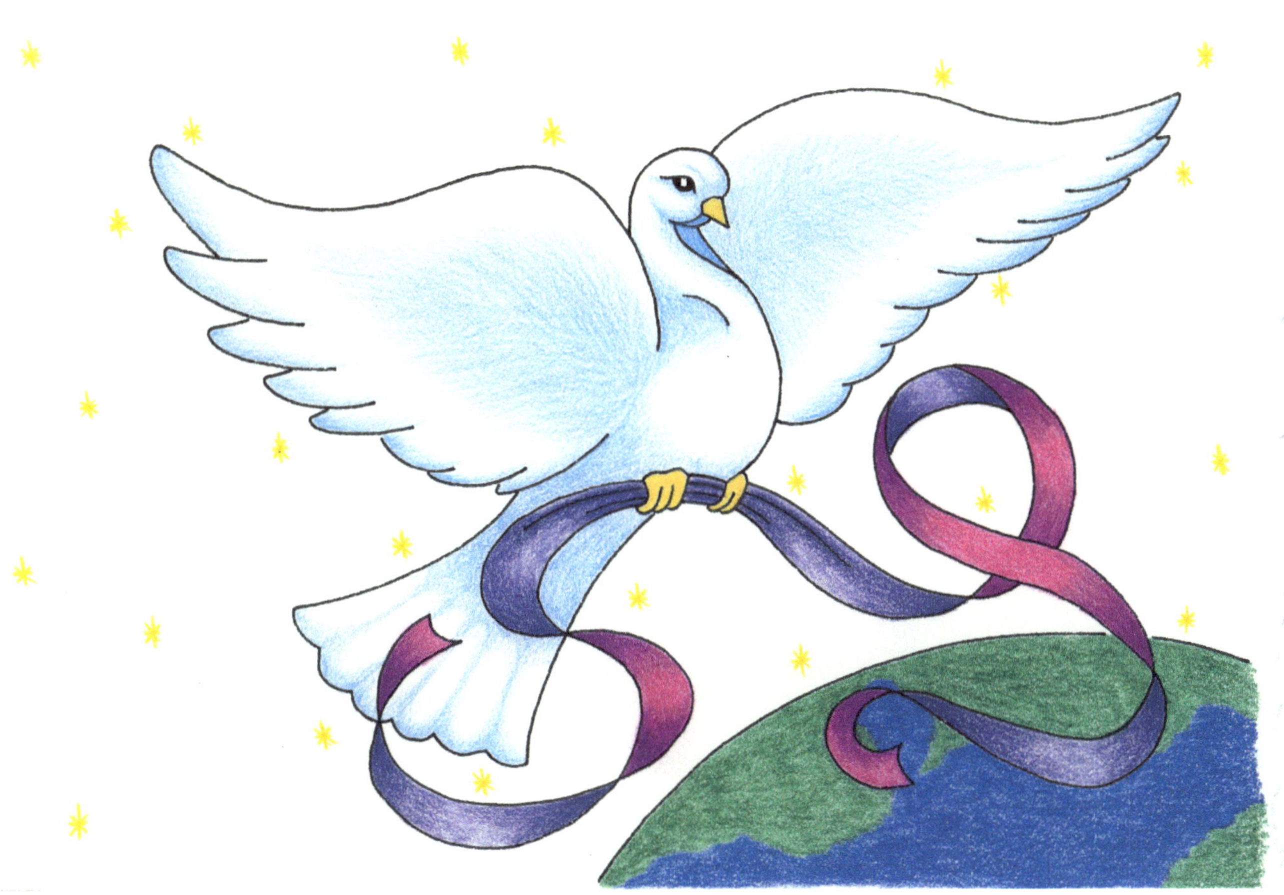

1998

# The Christmas Sparrow

2014

On a long ago Christmas Eve a bird, late in flying south, saw an impossible thing. Flustered, he landed in a wood near a city and went to a cottage with a warm hearth and a mad old woman and a beautiful young girl.

The woman was a witch.

The girl was something else.

The bird looked through the cottage window and saw the girl locked away alone in her room, away from the warmth of the fire, away from the company of the witch, away even from herself.

Shivering, she stared out the frosted window and saw a most remarkable, impossible thing: a snow sparrow, which does not exist, looking in. She opened the window. The bird gave her his coat of feathers to warm her. There seemed to be so few on such a small bird, but they expanded to be enough for the girl. She said, "I've seen an impossible thing."

"So have I," said the bird.

When the witch heard this, she grew angry. She cast the girl out into the cold of midnight on that long ago Christmas Eve, and she magicked the bird so that his featherless wings became like arms and his head sprouted hair. Then she gave him a name to ground him to the earth and cast him, too, into the night, with money enough for a train ticket and nothing more.

He traveled south. The money didn't take him far, so he wasn't always able to travel by train and was often stranded in a single place for months at a time. On Christmas Eve, he would search the sky for an impossible thing, and he stayed alive by trading his tales for hot chocolate.

One Christmas Eve, he came to a bar in a southern town, shivering from the cold. Even in the south the cold can penetrate your hollow bones. The patrons, the night before Christmas, were also lost, but they had for this night found each other and that was enough. They traded stories and warm drinks until the stroke of midnight, when a great many of them bowed their heads. He, however, looked up – though he saw only a stone ceiling and wood rafters.

The door burst open, and a woman stood there: tall and stately and severe, with raven hair and ruby lips and a coat of gorgeous white feathers. She extended her hand to him – he'd been spinning his stories and drinking cocoa through the night. She said, "Long ago, I saw an impossible thing."

"So did I."

"You," she said, "are my impossible thing."

Only then did he recognize her, so many years since his last flight. "You are my shivering girl." She smiled, but the smile wasn't meant for the bartenders or the lost souls in the room; it wasn't meant for anyone else but him. She shrugged out of the coat and offered it to him. Even as he touched it, the feathers seemed to glow, and there were somehow enough for his wings and the coat as well. The curse was broken, and the witch, far away and older, was glad of it.

"Let me show you my impossible thing," the snow sparrow said. "Let me take you north, to where the stars are brightest and the reindeer fly."

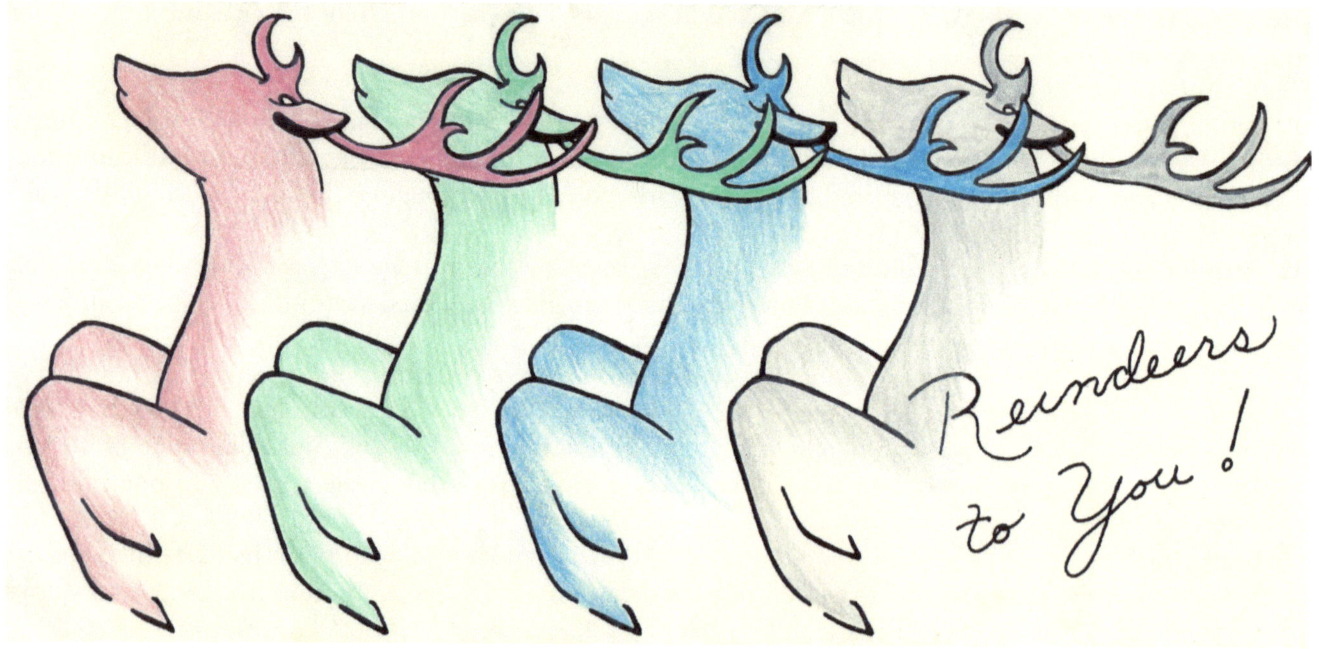
Reindeers
to You!

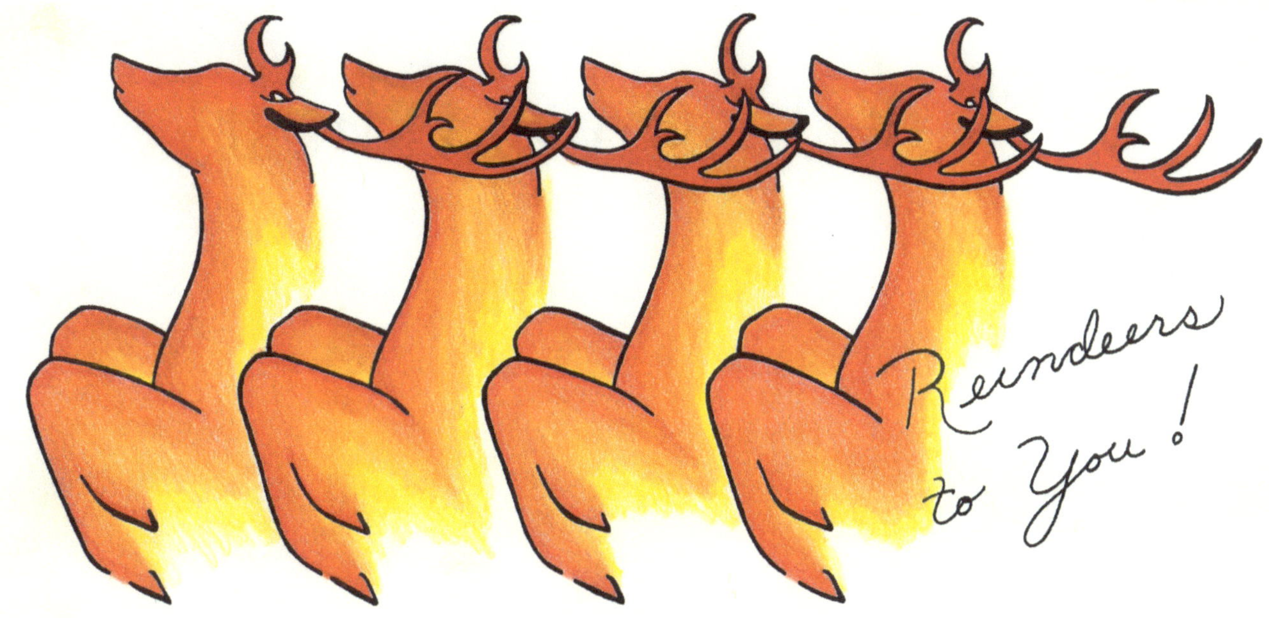


1986

# The Christmas Ghost

2015

The ghost arrives late. Three, even four full strokes after midnight and finally he shows up, a sack full of presents his excuse. He sets to handing out gifts immediately, without ceremony, without any introduction or segue, without any go-ahead from The Big Guy.

Everybody knows you can't have a Christmas Party without a Christmas Ghost, so of course they all laugh it off and ignore the transgression.

But I can't. It's the worst part of my job, the sacking of ghosts. They have a habit of sticking around and haunting you. But Christmas Ghosts are notoriously bad at hauntings. They'll pop an ornament off the tree and people blame the cat instead. They tend to think clinking chain sounds are scary, but the truth is: that's very nineteenth century.

So I call him over. "Ralph," I say, because it's my job to know all the Christmas Ghosts by name, "we need to talk."

Ralph doesn't know hòw to do anything but smile, so he puts more effort into it and hands me a present box. "Merry Christmas," he tells me.

"Ralph," I say, putting a friendly arm around the Christmas Ghost's shoulders. "You know the importance of spectacle and symbolism."

"I do," Ralph says. "You taught me that."

He gives me too much credit. "And anticipation," I add. "Expectation. Tradition."

"It's about the clock, isn't it?"

"It's about the clock."

The Christmas Ghost asks, "Can I say two things in my defense?"

"Sure."

"First, you taught me anticipation, and it never hurts to let a thing like that stretch just a little bit longer, does it, boss?"

I don't answer because, although he's right, in this case he's also wrong.

"Second," the Christmas Ghost says, "our host's magnificent grandfather clock is running almost a full four seconds fast."

I check my precision-timed watch, then the grandfather clock, then my watch again. He's right.

Which, for me, is a relief. "Merry Christmas, Ralph," I say, and I pull a gift from my pocket and hand it to him. "You're the best Christmas Ghost I know."

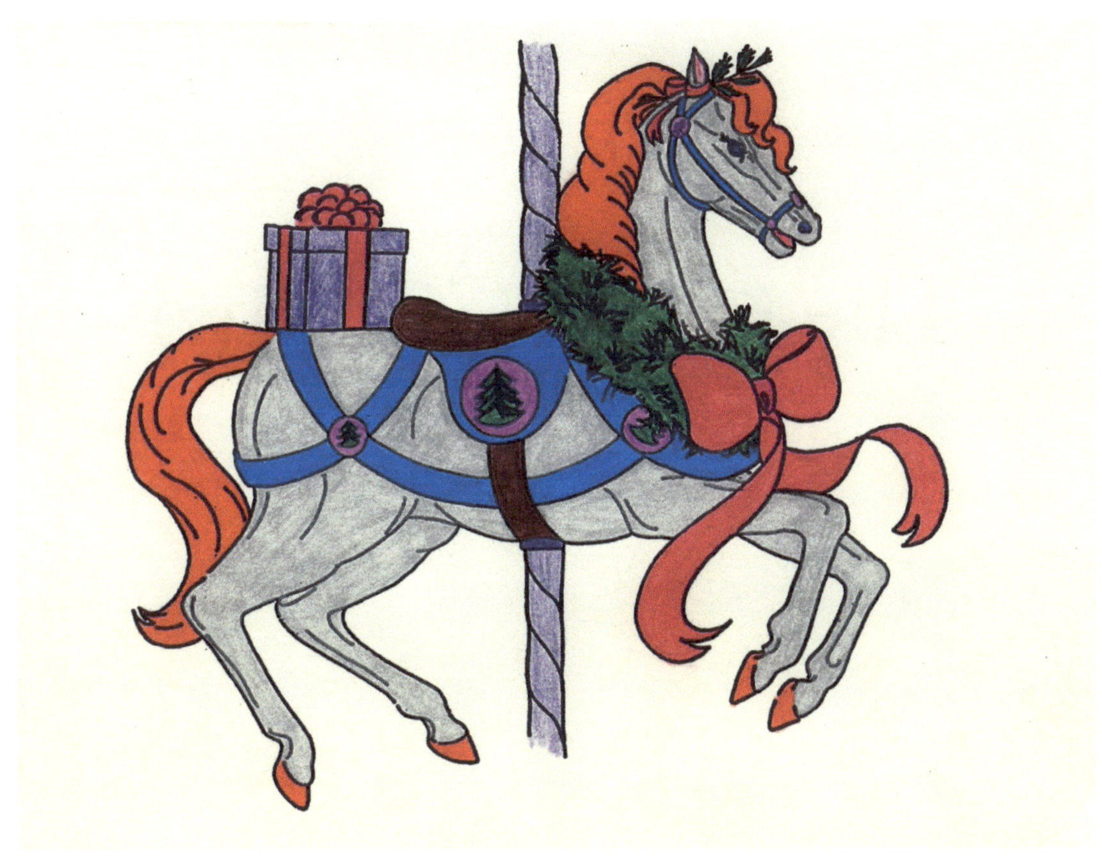

1988

# The Cat at Christmas

2016

The cat, perched upon the arm of a couch, watches her family of servants stringing lights and hanging glitzies and wrapping packages. She eyes the ribbons patiently, swishing her tail, waiting for just the right moment when a back is turned – then pounces.

She is pushed away, but not before the dancing ribbon, and all the threat it entails, has been shred to – well, ribbons.

The cat does not long ponder this mystery, and instead cleans herself so as to be presentable when next some sort of threat emerges.

The family is making food, what the cat has come to accept as their food, though it is not just meat but other things – some of which she has sampled and found at least intriguing. She hops onto the counter to offer assistance – to check for poisons, to approve the cuts of ham.

She is brushed aside, right off the counter, but not before she gets a taste of the meal, which she decides is too sweet anyway. They open a can for her, cat-friendly vittles, and she is at least temporarily satisfied.

Distant members of the family arrive, and will be disbursed throughout the house on all the beds and couches, and in blankets on the floors. Some of these visitors smell awful. They will take her favorite blankets, and she doesn't know where she'll sleep tonight – but they haven't disturbed all her hidey holes.

The visitors insist on cat hugs and cat kisses, which she endures to a certain point before scrambling free. She finds a new perch, swishes her tail, waits for their meal to culminate with singing. And after they've all gone to bed, she checks each corner of the house, and on the well-being of every resident and every guest, then turns her attentions to the tree.

She bats at the ornaments. She massages herself against its low hanging branches. She's about to climb, to chase after that angel at the very top, when there's movement.

But everyone was snug and sleeping.

It's another visitor, this one in red. He jingles and his belly jiggles as he piles wrapped packages beneath the tree. She does not crouch for attack; the big man poses no threat. She swishes her tail.

When he's done with the tree, and also the stockings, he bends low to look straight into the cat's eyes. He says, so she can understand, "I haven't forgotten you." Then he flicks a mouse – a fake little mouse with fake white fur and a long ribbon of a tail.

And just like that, the tree is forgotten in favor of prey, and another Christmas is saved.

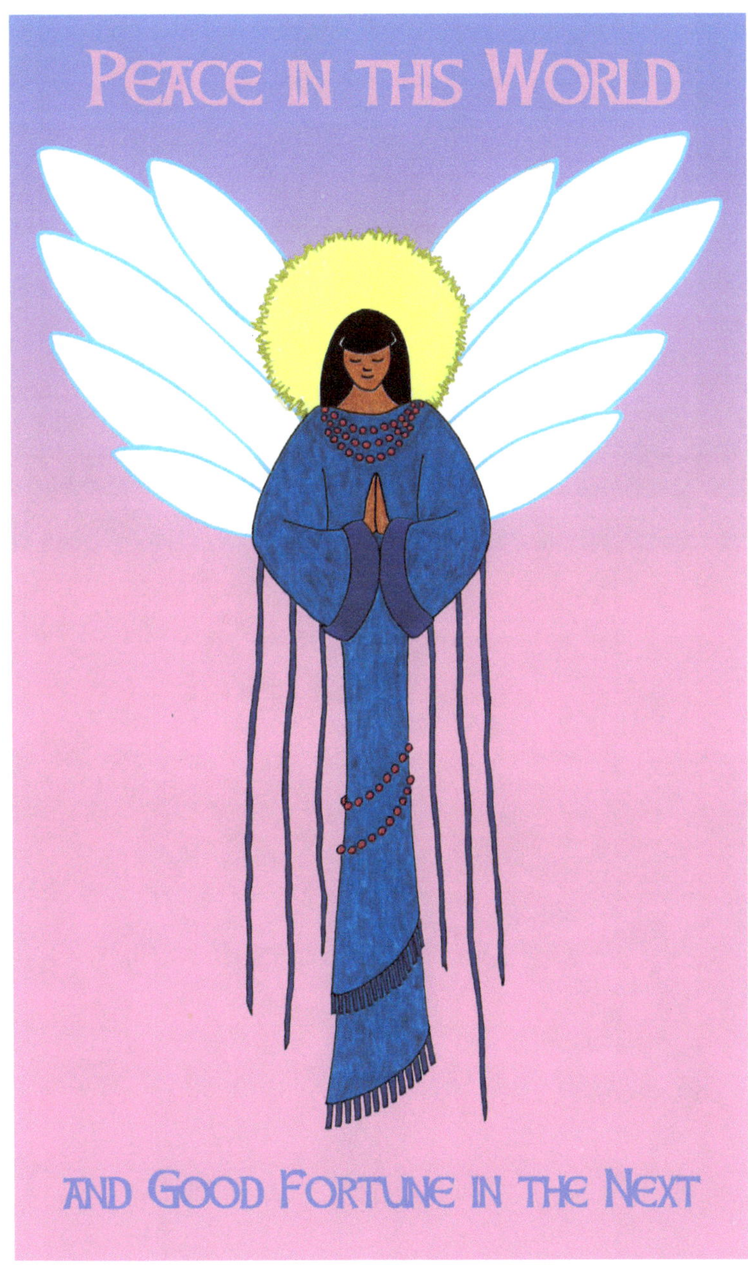


2007

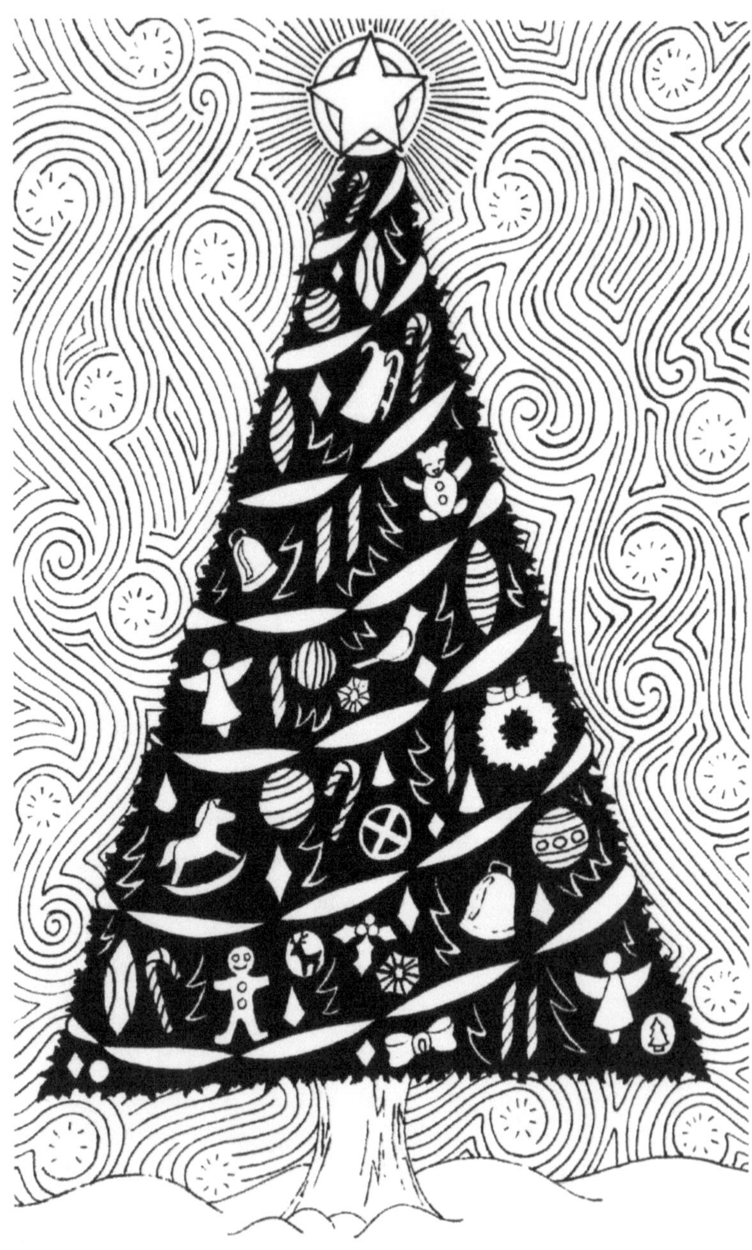

2015

# AFTERWORD

Once upon a time, a boy met a girl, and a great many things followed. But this is neither an Adventure nor a Romance. This is merely a collection of snapshots, artistic and literary, illustrating Christmases past. A visit, you might say, from one of the ghosts. So it doesn't matter, boy and girl – what matters is artist and writer.

I have no idea how it started. The artist in this tale had gotten her initial inspiration long before she met the writer, and he was inspired to do something similar. Other writers have done it before, one year or another, and inarguably, other writers have done it better, but none of them would have told my stories. And no other artists would have made what my artist created.

Maybe the truth is, this is a Romance of some sort. As the writer in this tale, as the boy, I was bitten – you might say by love, you might even say by my own personal muse.

After the first story, I wrote a second the next year, then another after that, until it became a tradition. And now, together, we – the artist and writer – pass that tradition on to you.

Whatever holiday you celebrate, please enjoy these. I hope its spirit lingers within you well past the season.

– John Urbancik
September 2016

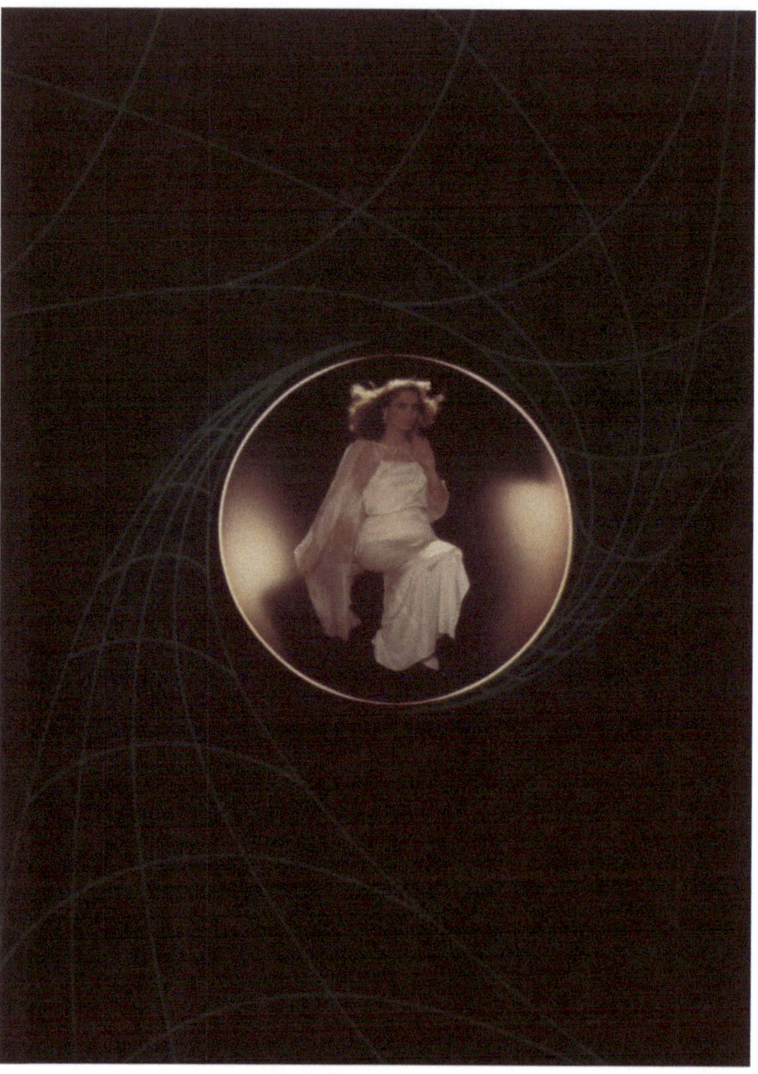

1984

# ABOUT THE AUTHOR

John Urbancik is an author of fantasy, dark fantasy, and horror–fairy tales and ghost stories. His first novel, *Sins of Blood and Stone*, was published in 2002. He is also the author of a series of collected stories called *InkStains*, a project in which he wrote a story a day every day for a year by hand. You can find him online at www.darkfluidity.com.

# ABOUT THE ARTIST

Mery-et Lescher (aka Mary Lescher) worked for 16 years with Disney Animation before returning to school to work on her Ph.D. in art history with a focus on animation and film history. She has lectured at The School of Visual Arts, taught classes at Florida State University, and worked as a curatorial assistant at the John and Mable Ringling Museum of Art.

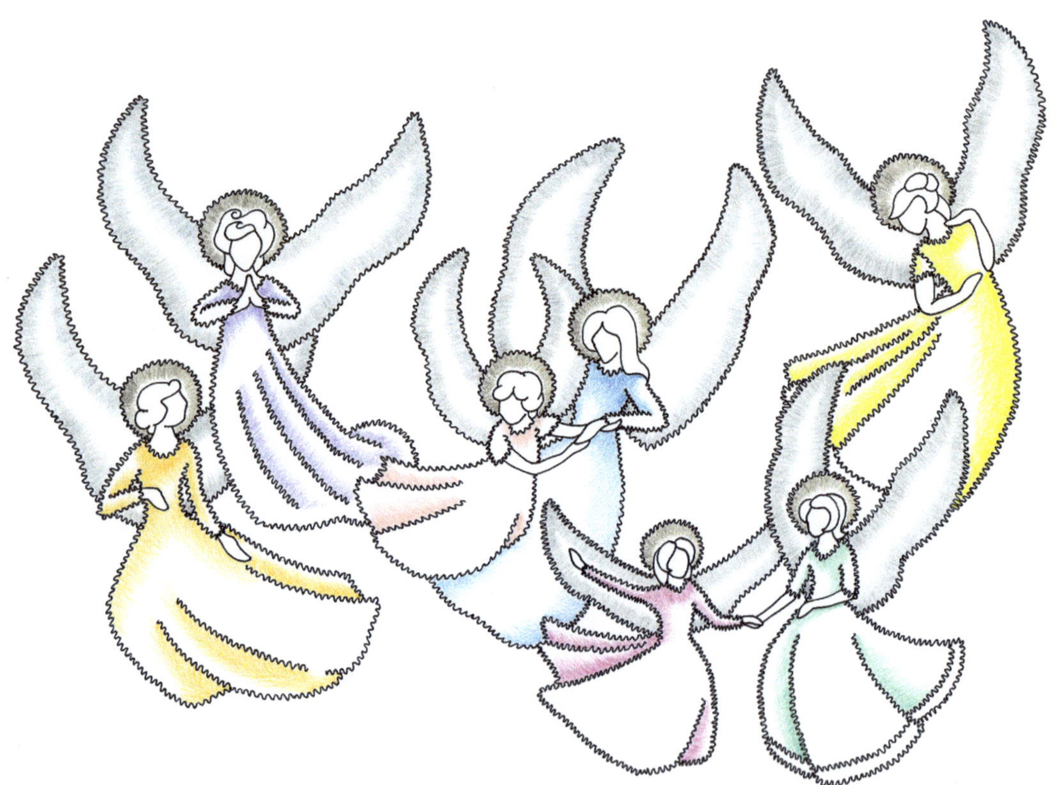

Preview: 2016
In Progress

www.ingramcontent.com/pod-product-compliance
Lightning Source LLC
LaVergne TN
LVHW070137110826
845147LV00002B/275

* 9 7 8 0 9 9 8 3 8 8 2 0 5 *